HORDE'S CHALLENGE

STARBARIAN SAGA BOOK ONE

ROBERT JESCHONEK

STARBARIAN SAGA BOOK ONE:
HORDE'S CHALLENGE

Published by Blastoff Books
411 Chancellor Street
Johnstown, Pennsylvania 15904

"These books are exciting and combine all the best things about science fiction with amazing plots! The stories are action-packed, with spaceships, battles, and aliens, but they still feature relatable characters. There are some really good plot twists that made me gasp when I first read them. If you love action and excitement, I highly recommend this series!"
– Ingrid Miller, Reviewer, Pittsburgh, PA

"Fun read! I love this thrilling space adventure series. With colorful worlds and even more colorful characters, it'll be hard to forget these epic novels. Get ready for a fully immersive experience."
– Sara Caskey, Reviewer, Providence, RI

"Robert Jeschonek has a flair for fast-paced, pulse-pounding combat scenes."
– William H. Keith, author of the *Grey Death Battlemech* novels

PART I

DEVILS BELOW

LIGHTNING FLASHED as the two blood-streaked broadswords crashed together, their razor-sharp blades gleaming in the blaze of light igniting the night sky.

Clang!

Boooom!

Thunder followed, mixing with the roars of the two heavily-muscled men fighting for supremacy in the heart of the storm. One pushed his sword forward, forcing the other's sword back--and then the other did the same, finding the strength to drive his opponent's weapon in the other direction.

They went at it like this for thrust after thrust, sweat-soaked muscles bunching and flexing in perfect balance. The men were too evenly matched for either one to seize victory and kill the other, though clearly, they were straining to do just that.

Their armies were doing exactly the same thing. On the muddy plain around them, their respective forces battled like maniacs, roaring and slashing and blud-geoning with a fervor that was at least the equal of the power of the storm that swirled around them. In their horned helmets, leather tunics, jagged spikes, and gleaming chains, they fought like the barbarians they were, the supreme warriors of a world that had long ago abandoned any pretense of civilization.

A world that was not now called anything at all, its once-proud name lost in the distant reaches of history.

Clang!

Again, the two men in the middle of the battle--the leaders of those armies--swung their swords together with crushing force. Again, the lightning flashed, and again, neither man could claim a decisive advantage. They both let loose roars of rage to the highest heavens, as if by that noise, one could somehow gain superiority over the other.

But the noise was not enough. The deadlock continued.

The opposing armies hacked away at each other, mowing down man after man and woman after woman--yet their numbers remained roughly the same. The two leaders swung and slashed their mighty swords, yet always they stayed on their feet and held their ground.

This test of wills and power was not going to end *anytime* soon...barring the unexpected.

Booom!

"Surrender!" Angar, the black-haired leader with the spiky silver helmet bound in black leather straps, hissed the word between clenched teeth. "Your so-called *warriors* are *gutted* and *broken*."

"*Your* wretched weaklings are the ones dropping like *flies.*" The second leader unleashed a flurry of moves that should have cut down his enemy in seconds...but he dodged every one of them. His helmet, which was topped with a winged, screaming skull, seemed to swoop right and left as he ducked and sidestepped, his shoulder-length blond hair flying. "Soon, the horde of *Tork Gallgore* will *rule* this land and *plunder* all its *treasures!*"

"Not while *Angar Crux* still lives to fight!" With a sudden feint and sweep of his head, Angar slashed with his helmet spikes at Tork's throat. But he missed when Tork flung around his sword and smashed the helmet aside.

Lightning flashed just as Tork slammed Angar down to the muck, sending his sword flying. Before the thunder followed, a downpour of rain suddenly burst from the clouds, drenching the plain in all directions.

WHOOOSHH

BABOOM

Just as Tork raised his broadsword, ready to plunge it into his opponent's chest, Angar lunged at him, knocking him back. This time, it was Tork's sword that flew as the two men dropped, wrestling desperately in the mud.

Rain continued to blast them as they fought, rolling and twisting and clawing to the sounds of screams and clanging weapons all around them. Every blow felt like a death blow, every hold felt like the end--yet Angar and Tork struggled on, too evenly matched for the tide to turn one way or the other.

"Yield!" shouted Tork. "Accept the doom you *deserve!*"

Angar's answer was to gather all his strength and flip

his opponent down brutally, then grab a nearby rock and raise it high. "*You* deserve doom! You deserve the *torture* and *terror* you've given so many helpless *people!*"

With a furious curse, Tork grabbed Angar's arm and kept it from swinging down at his head with the rock. He forced it back suddenly, aimed right at Angar's head, intending to smash it to a bloody pulp.

Again, lightning flashed.

WA-BOOOOMM

The rock shook as both men jockeyed for control. Again, they were deadlocked, trapped in a stalemate, unable to break the balance and push everything one way or the other.

Then, suddenly, they were bathed in a bright red flare. Their struggle didn't end, but they both turned their gazes up into the flickering light.

This time, it had nothing to do with lightning. What they saw hovering over them was the figure of a man robed in bright yellow flame. Seemingly unaffected by the pouring rain, he stared down at them with flashing, burning eyes. Somehow, he was not consumed by the fire, though it engulfed him entirely except for his bronzed face, hands, and feet.

Because they had met his kind before, the men knew exactly what he was, though his reasons for being there escaped them both. That in itself wasn't unusual...though he didn't keep them guessing for long.

"ANGAR CRUX! TORK GALLGORE!" The fire-robed man's voice boomed louder than the thunder, making his words heard all across the plain and beyond. "HOW MANY TIMES HAS IT BEEN?"

For once, Angar and Tork's gazes met without hostile intent. They scowled, wondering what the burning man meant and what he wanted.

"ONE HUNDRED? ONE THOUSAND?" The fire-cloaked man spread his arms wide, releasing sparks and ashes to swirl up into the sky. "HOW MANY TIMES HAVE YOU *TRIED* AND *FAILED* TO *DESTROY* EACH OTHER?"

"*I* will not *fail* this time!" snapped Angar, clenching his teeth and pushing the rock harder toward Tork. "By the searing winds of *Kromathon,* I *swear* I will *annihilate* him this time!"

"SWEAR ALL YOU LIKE, BUT WE BOTH KNOW THE TRUTH!" The Blacksmith raised his arms higher, and his flames flared brighter. "NEITHER OF YOU CAN WIN AGAINST THE OTHER! YOUR ENDLESS WAR IS HOPELESS!"

"What do *you* know, Blacksmith?" said Angar. "When did *you* last win a *war?*"

"*THIS MORNING!*" roared the Blacksmith.

As the echoes of his voice died down, so too did the cacophony of battle on the plain. The clanging of iron and howls of rage and pain faded; Tork and Angar suddenly realized that all their fighters were listening closely to every word from the burning man.

"BELIEVE ME WHEN I SAY, I CAN HELP *ONE OF YOU* WIN *YOUR* WAR, TOO."

"*How?*" Angar and Tork said in unison.

"A CONTEST. TOMORROW." The Blacksmith's flaming cloak rippled in the wind and rain but never went out. "THE WINNER WILL RECEIVE A MYSTICAL

WEAPON THAT WILL FINALLY BREAK THIS IMPASSE."

"Im--pass?" Angar frowned.

"THE WINNER WILL BE UNSTOPPABLE," said the Blacksmith. "THE LOSER WILL BE DEAD."

Angar and Tork's eyes widened, never doubting it could be so. The Blacksmiths had a long history of using their magic to perform the impossible.

But the details of the contest were still important. "Tell us *more* about this contest and weapon," said Tork. "How will they both work?"

"YOU HAVE UNTIL SUNRISE TOMORROW TO ACCEPT," said the Blacksmith. "THAT IS *ALL* YOU NEED TO KNOW."

"Accept *how?*" snarled Angar.

"TELL A FIRE," said the Blacksmith. "WE WILL KNOW."

With that, he suddenly spun and disappeared in a whirl of flaming tongues. Glowing yellow embers swam away from the spot where he'd been, hissing out in the drenching downpour and falling as sodden ashes to the mud.

Angar and Tork looked at each other, then looked around at their waiting armies. If they had until sunrise to accept the challenge, that still left ample time to finish the battle, didn't it?

Before they could say a word, however, a vortex of flame whipped to life in the air above them, becoming the very Blacksmith who'd disappeared moments ago.

"AND SHUT DOWN THIS BATTLE WHILE YOU'RE AT IT," he said, "OR THE DEAL'S *OFF.*"

Tork sighed. "You heard him!" he shouted at the top of his lungs. "The battle's over!"

"End it!" roared Angar.

Without argument or hesitation, everyone on the plain lowered their weapons and stepped away from whatever mayhem they'd been about to resume.

"SUNRISE TOMORROW!" said the Blacksmith. "AND IF EITHER ONE OF YOU BACKS OUT, THE OTHER ONE AUTOMATICALLY GETS THE WEAPON!"

Then, in another flurry of flame, the Blacksmith was gone again. Lightning flashed when he disappeared, as if it had been somehow triggered by his passage.

BA-BOOOM!

For a moment after that, Angar and Tork remained locked together as before, the rock still raised between them. One gave it a token push, then the other.

And then both slowly lowered it to the muddy ground.

"I don't like this," said Angar as he slowly got to his feet. "I *hate* Blacksmiths and their stinking *deals.*"

Tork shrugged as he also stood. "But imagine the *reward* if it works out. One of us finally *triumphs* over the other."

"Sure, but I keep thinking." Angar retrieved his broadsword from the muck and swung it in a skillful figure-eight. "What does *he* get out of it?"

"The Blacksmith?"

Angar nodded. "Why is *that* bastard making this offer to us *hordesmen?*"

"Does it matter?" said Tork.

"It might." Angar slid his sword into the sheath on his back. "Neither of us can possibly say *no*, can we?"

"I don't know." Tork thought for a moment. "It seems like a *cowardly* way to *destroy* you, doesn't it?"

"If it means final *revenge* for your *crimes?*" Angar curled his lip in a hateful sneer. "*Any* way would make *me* feel good."

"Assuming the Blacksmith is true to his word." Tork retrieved his own sword and wiped the mud from the blade on his tunic. "Think about it."

"Think about what?"

"Why would a Blacksmith give either of *us* a weapon with the power to *destroy?*"

Angar snorted. "Remind me to ask him after I'm done slaughtering *you* with it."

"*You* will die *first,* scum!" shouted Tork, and then he whipped around and marched off across the rain-swept plain, storming through the darkness like a leviathan diving into the deep.

2

FOR A MAN LIKE ANGAR CRUX, the horde he commanded was his family, and its camp was his home.

The blasting rain meant nothing as he marched through it after his encounter with the Blacksmith. As soon as the brown tents of his people came into view, he felt a surge of joy and relief.

This was his purpose in life. Everything he did was driven by his need to protect and enrich these nomadic warriors. Everything he wanted and fought for could be found within the walls of these battered animal-skin tents.

Except for the one thing no one but the Blacksmith could provide, if indeed that fiery sorcerer was telling anything remotely resembling the truth about tomorrow's contest.

Did that one thing outweigh all the rest? Was murdering his archenemy, Tork, worth risking his own future and that of everyone and everything he cared about?

Maybe his wives would have the answer.

"Husband!" Vixa ran from the tent they shared, long black hair streaming behind her. "Let us *seal* the fate of hated Angar! The fire is *stoked* and ready for you to accept the Blacksmith's challenge!"

Word of the contest had traveled fast, though the burning man's visit had happened only moments ago.

"You approve, then?" asked Angar.

"Why wouldn't I?" Vixa wrapped her arms around his soaked, bloody body and grinned darkly. "Final victory over that *scum* will fulfill your greatest dream and guarantee your dominance over *all* the wander-lands!"

"*Or* it's a *trap.*" Redheaded Peri, as usual, seemed to appear out of nowhere, without warning. Her deep green eyes locked onto Angar from inches away. "These Blacksmiths are *not* to be trusted."

"You want him to miss the opportunity to *crush* his foe?" Vixa laughed cruelly. "Perhaps you want *Tork* to triumph instead?"

"I remember how the Blacksmiths tricked my father and his men," said Peri. "They made *promises*, and then they used their *magic* to drive them out of their own *lands.*"

"I know all *about* the Blacksmiths' promises!" snapped Vixa. "And I know that as often as they *ruin* a man, they might also make him a *king!*"

"And can you *predict* when *that* will happen?" Peri leaned closer, and her eyes flashed with icy fury. "Can *anyone* predict what the *Blacksmiths* will do?"

Just then, Angar's third wife, Reyel, stormed toward them with two babies in her arms. As beautiful as she was, with flowing blonde hair and delicate features, she was known far and wide as the most savage of the three women.

"*I'll* do it!" she shouted. "Let *me* take your place in the contest!"

Vixa frowned. "Can she *do* that?"

"Enough!" Angar broke free of Vixa's embrace and backed away from all three women. They were hard to take sometimes, even for a Horde Lord, even when the *other four* wives weren't around. "I need to think!"

Vixa's frown deepened. "What is there to *think* about? You have a chance to kill Tork, you *take* it!"

"Maybe," said Peri.

"Why, 'maybe?'" asked Reyel.

"I'm just saying." Peri raised her eyebrows and shrugged. "We don't know the exact rules of the *contest* yet, do we?"

Everyone fell silent. Angar shook his head.

"What if it's something that gives *the Traitor* an advantage?" asked Peri. "Then what?"

"Not possible!" shouted Reyel, and both babies started crying loudly.

"But what if it is?" said Peri.

"Then you *cheat*," said Vixa, and she laughed. "None of your *honor* shit *this* time. Not with the *stakes* so high."

All three women chattered at once, then, all telling him what he should do. He let it roll for one long moment, and then he'd had enough.

"*Shut up!*" Angar roared out the words so loudly, even the crying babies fell silent. "I am *lord* of this *horde! I* make the decisions here! *You* will all do as you're told!"

The three women lowered their eyes--some more reluctantly than others. As overbearing as they could be at times, they still acknowledged his authority over them and all the tribesmen of the Eastern Horde.

"Now one of you bring me *food!*" commanded Angar. "Another bring me *drink!* And the *other* tend my *wounds.* When I have had my *fill* and made up my *mind,* you will *know* my *choice!*"

As if in response, one of the babies started bawling again...then stopped suddenly when it caught him scowling at it.

"Get moving!" Angar smacked Vixa on the bottom, earning a deep-seated scowl of his own. "Or do you *want* me to let Tork win and take the lot of you as his personal *property?*"

3

WHEN TORK GALLGORE entered his camp on the opposite side of the plain from Angar's, it was like wading through a field of tall grass. His tribe, the people of the Southern Horde, parted around him, moving aside to let him go where he must go.

He dropped his weapons and stripped off his clothing as he went, letting it fall without regard. The hands of his loyal subjects lifted it away without a word--the broadsword and scabbard, the spiked helmet with black straps, the metal plating and chains, the leather boots and tunic. His people, as always, were like an extension of him, anticipating and serving as if their minds were linked to his.

By the time he reached the medicine tent, he was naked, as he had to be. Even the lord of all the horde was not permitted to bring the things of the outside world into that sacred place.

Lifting open the entry flap, Tork saw the tent was already full of hazy smoke. The Blessed had known he would come, then, and lit the fire of herbs and incense in preparation.

"Father, Mother," he said as he pushed inside, though the old man and woman in the tent were not his parents. "The death of my greatest foe is within my grasp."

"We know this," said Father. "Messengers brought us the news."

"You may speak to the flames when you choose." Mother's bony face tightened in a smile, a cryptic rictus. Like Tork and Father, she was completely naked. "Or you may hold your tongue for as long as you like."

"Thank you, Mother. Father." Tork sat on a black fur by the fire. "I come seeking *visions.*"

"Then *breathe deep.*" Mother chuckled. "The stuff of visions is all *around* us."

Tork closed his eyes and did as she said, drawing the acrid smoke down into his lungs. It wouldn't be long until the visions came; he had sought them many times before and knew the process well.

"Let it *fill* you," chanted Father. "Let it *take* you."

"Let it *show* you," said Mother. "Let it *tell* you."

Tork swayed softly in the haze. His mind began to swirl--gently at first--with colors and light.

Eventually, the colors and light resolved themselves into images--but he could barely understand them. He saw starry darkness...unfamiliar faces...strange creatures who looked more like *beasts* than *people.* He saw flames and explosions, flying debris--heard thunder and screams and all manner of violent noise. So much of it like nothing he had ever seen or dreamed before...and yet there was also *blood*, and *pain*, and *death*. *Those* things, at least, he knew quite well.

But through it all, a thread ran strong and clear-- something else familiar amid the strangeness. Though it was something he had not *felt* in quite a while, had not experienced in what seemed like a lifetime, he recognized it instantly.

It was enough to make his heart hammer furiously in his chest. *Fear.*

And somehow, he knew: it would all be part of his future if he took the Blacksmith up on his offer.

At least, that was what the smoke was telling him.

"You have seen it, haven't you?" asked Father.

"You have *known* it, haven't you?" asked Mother.

Tork opened his eyes and nodded. "But I don't *understand.*"

"That is often the case," said Father.

"And I did not *see* another *path.*" Tork frowned. "I still don't know if what I've seen is the *better* fate, or the *worse.*"

"Perhaps it is the *only* fate allowed you." Mother cackled. "Perhaps you have not seen another path because *no* other path is *permitted.*"

"It happens," said Father. "When someone has a *special* role that cannot be *denied.*"

"You're telling me that no matter what *choice* I make, my *fate* will be the same?" Tork's eyes widened with growing rage. "You're saying that *I*, the *Lord* of the *Southern Horde*, have no *control* over my own *destiny?*"

Father bowed his head and spread his arms. "We have no *answer* for that, Lord. The *visions* are the *visions.*"

"But a special fate is not always a *curse,*" said Mother. "It can be the greatest blessing you have ever known, no matter how troubling the visions you have glimpsed of it."

"Bah!" Tork shot to his feet. "You speak *nonsense.*"

Suddenly, he felt a wave of dizziness and slipped out of the moment. He found himself in another vision, the clearest he'd ever experienced.

He knelt on a cold, hard surface spattered with blood. His hands were clenched around the throat of another man, tightening...choking the breath and life out of him.

Men and women screamed all around. There were booms and crashes and flashes of light--high-pitched shrieks, the wailing of some kind of horn. The air was filled with the reek of blood and offal, the stench of smoke.

The surface rumbled and pitched, but he never let go. Something hit him from behind, clubbing the back of his skull, and he only clenched his grip harder.

And he grinned. Because the man he was strangling was Angar Crux.

Die! He barked the word in his vision. *Die for what you have done!*

And then, suddenly, he was back in the medicine tent, only he was the one lying on the floor. Father and Mother gazed down at him through the haze, looking concerned.

"Lord?" asked Mother. "Are you all right?"

The back of Tork's head hurt. He must have hit it when he'd fallen.

But he didn't mention it. The memory of his last vision was so fresh in his mind, all he could do was smile.

"He's all right." Father smiled back at him. "He saw something wonderful, didn't he?"

Tork sat up. "I know what I'm going to do," he told them. "Now get that fire stoked. The Blacksmith is waiting for my answer."

4

ANGAR SAT on a stone by the fire on the edge of camp, watching the softly flickering flames. Everyone else in the Eastern Horde was asleep except the sentries, who knew enough to keep their distance from the troubled horde lord.

The horizon was brightening faintly, meaning Angar's time was almost up. If he wanted to participate in the Blacksmith's contest, he had to give his answer soon. It would be too late once the sun rose, and he would forfeit victory to Tork if Tork accepted the offer.

Still, Angar continued to hesitate. Even after worrying about it all night, he couldn't seem to resolve the knot of doubt tied deep in his soul.

Every time he thought he had it worked out, he hesitated. He knew what he *should* do, what he *wanted* to do, but something kept holding him back.

That kind of uncertainty wasn't like him at all. As a leader, he was known for brash, quick decision-making that always worked out for the best. As a fighter, he was known for unbeatable speed and coordination that had never been beaten--only deadlocked by the bane of his existence, Tork.

Whatever the problem was, he knew it didn't matter much anymore. He couldn't just sit back and let Tork accept the invitation--and the weapon that would grant him ultimate victory. Even if Tork *didn't* take up the Blacksmith on his offer--*especially* then--Angar would be a *fool* not to jump at it.

He *had* to do it, and he knew it. It was the only choice that made sense...so *why* was he waiting until the last minute to make it?

A *feeling*. That was why. An indefinable *feeling* that he was about to make a terrible mistake.

And even now, with it staring him in the face, he didn't understand *why* and what was *really* at stake.

"Don't do it."

Angar jumped at the sound of Peri's voice suddenly whispering in his ear. She was the only person he'd ever met who could sneak up on him like that. *"Run away* like a *child* and avoid whatever *frightens* you."

"Nothing frightens me!" snapped Angar.

"Not even the *sun* rising over the horizon?" Peri pointed at the brightening sky across the corpse-strewn plain. Any second now, the sun was going to top it.

Angar snorted. "Of course not."

"Then what about *them?"* Leaning back, she gestured in the direction of camp.

When Angar looked, he saw the entire Eastern Horde

in all its glory marching toward him, heavily armed and led by Vixa and Reyel.

"They come to support you in the contest," said Peri. "Shall *I* tell them you won't be entering it?"

Angar growled deep in his throat and turned to the fire. Even as the sun's glow grew in the distance, he spoke into the guttering flames as if they were some kind of living thing.

"I accept your challenge, Blacksmith," he said. "And I will *win.*"

"Good for you, my love." Peri kissed him on the cheek as the sun finally rose. "Now I wonder *where* this contest is going to *happen?*"

Just as she finished the question, a huge wedge of purple light appeared on the far edge of the battlefield, accompanied by a shuddering hum. As Angar watched, the wedge lurched forward, plowing through the remains of the previous day's battle with ease. Muck and corpses dissolved when it touched them, turning into steam...leaving behind a smooth, black surface, gleaming and free of debris.

"I think I can take a *guess.*" Angar smirked, though he wasn't much in the mood for joking around. "At least we won't have far to travel."

"We'll all have a short walk back to camp," said Peri, "if we need to make water or whatever."

"That's funny." Angar laughed. "Like we all won't just *piss* on the *spot*, being *barbarians* and all."

"I like the way you think." Peri chuckled and reached out to smooth his hair. "That idiot *Tork* doesn't stand a *chance* against you."

Angar felt a surge of lingering doubt and forcefully pushed it down again. "When I *crush* him, we will drink the *marrow* from his *bones*, you and I."

"Better yet, let's feed it to the dogs." She smiled as she kissed him on the lips. "You and I can feast on *Blacksmith* marrow instead."

They both looked at the fire at the same time, as if suddenly worried the Blacksmiths might hear them through it...and then they laughed and kissed some more.

Even though, in his deepest heart of hearts, Angar never really stopped worrying about what he'd gotten himself in for.

5

BANKS OF CLOUDS rolled away overhead just as Tork led the Southern Horde to the challenge place, releasing the sun and its bright beams to flare upon the polished black surface.

Seeing the sun emerge like that made Tork feel proud and fearless, as if it were a sign that he was destined to triumph. He squared his shoulders on either side of his broadsword scabbard and marched faster, eager to begin the contest. The sooner he won, the sooner he'd receive the weapon and use it to annihilate Angar.

The vision from the medicine tent left no doubt in his mind that he would claim his enemy's life in the end. His confidence was high and the outcome assured. Whatever challenge awaited on that field at the hands of the Black-smiths, he knew he would be victorious.

Having the full support of his people behind him only made him feel stronger and more invincible. They stormed toward the field as if into battle, waving swords and spears and torches high. He knew they would do anything they could to ensure his triumph.

Just as the horde swarming up to the opposite side of the field would do the same for *their* lord. Equal in size and armament, more or less, to Tork's army, the Eastern Horde poured up from its camp and arrayed itself along the field's edge. Like the Southern Horde, they waved their swords and spears in support of their own leader, who stood at the middle and a little way in front of the line.

When Angar and his supporters drew closer and took up position on their own side of the field, things really turned raucous. Tork's people wailed and shook their weapons, shouting out taunts and threats. Angar's followers tried their best to outdo them, blasting insults and obscenities at the Southerners.

As always happened before a confrontation, the two sides waged a war of intimidation without a single blow being thrown. They pounded their chests and stomped their feet, flung out their tongues and screeched like animals. They rhythmically chanted promises of pain and suffering, sang of the indignities they would inflict upon each other. They growled and barked and made faces so awful and demented that they could have come from some kind of otherworldly monsters or demons.

The whole time, Tork and Angar stood stock-still and stared at each other across the field, never breaking eye contact. It was as if each thought he could, through sheer force of will, bring down the other without lifting a single finger.

How many times had they faced each other like this,

the blood pounding in their ears as the hordes roared around them? How many times had they walked to the precipice like this, expecting to push each other over once and for all? Too many to count--but this time, to Tork, felt different. This time, the roaring chants and stomping feet and shaking weapons seemed more stirring than ever.

And not just because of the visions. Everything felt *amplified* somehow, larger than life. The Blacksmiths--believed to be agents of the gods themselves--made it all seem *grand* and *portentous* and *magical*.

They appeared in midair around the field when the hordes had gathered, forming a ring at least as high as three stacked standing men. Each of them burned with a different color of flame--yellow, red, orange, blue, green, purple, white. When they spread their arms, the flames flared brighter, illuminating the polished field even as the sun disappeared behind a swell of black clouds.

When the flames of the Blacksmiths brightened, the hordes stopped chanting and dancing. All eyes turned upward, awaiting whatever incredible things would happen next...whatever spectacle would dazzle them and provide meat for the songs and stories they would sing and tell in years to come.

"SO IT BEGINS!" The Blacksmith wrapped in yellow flames--the one who'd appeared during the battle the night before--was the first to speak. His voice echoed over the field, reaching everyone who stood and listened on all sides. "THE CONTEST TO PROVE WHICH OF YOUR LEADERS IS FIT TO BE LORD OF ALL THE HORDES."

The crowd roared with excitement, the Eastern and Southern hordes fighting to drown each other out.

Even with all that tumult, the Blacksmith's voice continued to come through loud and clear. "THE RULES ARE SIMPLE. THE MAN WHO SLAYS THE DRAGON WINS. HE WILL BE GIVEN A WEAPON THAT WILL ENABLE HIM TO KILL ALL HIS ENEMIES AND DOMINATE THE WORLD."

Again, the crowd roared.

"ONLY THESE TWO CAN COMPETE." When the Blacksmith pointed at Tork and Angar, bright spots of light made each of them stand out from the crowd. "IF ANYONE ELSE ENTERS THE PROVING GROUND, THAT ONE'S LORD WILL FORFEIT THE PRIZE."

This time, the crowd mostly groaned in disappointment.

"THE TWO FIGHTERS MAY USE ANY WEAPONS THEY CARRY ONTO THE FIELD BEFORE THE CONTEST BEGINS," said the Blacksmith. "THEY MAY *NOT* RECEIVE *NEW* WEAPONS *DURING* THE MATCH. AND THEY MAY *NOT* DIRECTLY ATTEMPT TO HARM *EACH OTHER*."

Again, the crowd's response was subdued.

"LASTLY," said the Blacksmith, "IF *NEITHER* MAN SLAYS THE DRAGON, *BOTH* HORDES SHALL BE ABANDONED TO ITS TENDER MERCIES. THE SLAUGHTER OF EVERY MAN, WOMAN, AND CHILD SHALL BE ALL BUT ASSURED."

The crowd was dead silent after *that* one.

"BUT WITH THESE BRAVE LEADERS OF YOURS IN THE FRAY, I AM SURE YOU HAVE *NOTHING* TO WORRY ABOUT," said the Blacksmith. "AND THERE *IS* SOMETHING *YOU* CAN DO TO *HELP* THEM WIN.

CHEER THEM ON EVERY STEP OF THE WAY AND THEY WILL FIGHT *HARDER."*

His words energized the crowd again. The hundreds of men, women, and children roared as one, as if they were all backing the same leader and hoping for the same outcome.

"AND NOW, THE TIME HAS COME!" The yellow-flamed Blacksmith left the others in the ring and glided smoothly to the middle of the field. "THE CONTES-TANTS WILL ENTER THE PROVING GROUND."

Tork grabbed a battle axe from one of his fighters and rushed forward, determined to take the initiative. Angar, already armed with a mace and broadsword, was only a step slower in jogging from the edge to the middle of the field.

"PREPARE TO STRUGGLE AGAINST THE DEAD-LIEST CREATURE EVER CONCEIVED ON THIS WORLD OR ANY OTHER!" The yellow Blacksmith rotated in place, turning his gaze from Tork to Angar and back again. "PREPARE FOR THE GREATEST BATTLE OF YOUR LIVES!"

Tork and Angar stood in the center of the field and glared at each other with all the hatred they could muster. It was almost as if they were there to fight each other to the death, not the dragon.

"AND NOW, LET THE CONTEST BEGIN!" As the Blacksmith said it, he and his colleagues whirled madly, shedding jets of colored flame. The jets spun together over the middle of the field, merging into a seething, crackling fireball that swiftly built in size and ferocity.

The Blacksmiths spun ever faster, and the fireball

became so big and bright that almost everyone in the crowd had to shield their eyes. *Still* it picked up speed and intensity with each passing second.

Then, finally, the Blacksmiths stopped spinning, and so did the fireball. It surged in size one last time, then imploded with a violent *boom*, leaving a huge *hole* gaping in the blue sky.

As Tork gazed into that hole, the hairs on the back of his neck stood up. He saw nothing but blackness in that cavity, the absence of life and form, and yet--something about it bothered him.

Suddenly, a deafening roar thundered out of that hole...then a piercing shriek.

RAAAAHHHHH! AYEEEEKKK!

Nothing could tear Tork's eyes from the hole at that point. He kept staring, waiting for a glimpse of whatever had made those cries. So did Angar, gripping the handles of his mace and broadsword so tightly, his knuckles whitened.

RAAAAHHHHH! AYEEEEKKK!

The cries were louder this time, yet still there was only blackness in the hole.

Then, a shape appeared in the darkness. It was a gleaming, obsidian shape moving toward the opening, getting bigger as it got closer. And it had *eyes*--fiery red eyes, three pairs of them--and round nostrils flashing on its front end in the shadows.

RAAAAHHHHH! AYEEEEKKK!

"HERE IT COMES!" said the Blacksmith. "GET READY FOR THE FIGHT OF YOUR LIVES!"

The crowd roared in unison. Tork stole a glance at

Angar, who happened to look his way at the same instant. A flicker of understanding passed between them.

Whatever was approaching, putting it down would be *no* easy task.

"SLAY IT!" said the Blacksmith. "WIN THE KEY TO YOUR ENEMY'S SLAUGHTER!"

Suddenly, the monstrosity burst free, and the hole collapsed in on itself. The thing was now revealed for all to see, its vast, gleaming bulk soaring down from the sky.

Tork had seen drawings of dragons before, heard tell of what they looked like and what they could do. The creature descending toward the field was every bit as powerful and terrifying as any of them.

It had a huge, lizard-like body with backswept fins and a long neck and tail. Its nostrils pulsed with crimson light, and the tip of its tail was barbed with spikes the length of a man. Its gargantuan wings were rigid and angled back, easily half the span of the field from tip to tip.

Swooping low over the field, it roared and shrieked again. The burning red glow in its nostrils flared as if it were about to breathe fire at the two men watching down below.

Otherwise, its only color was the black of death, infused in every glossy, metallic scale from the tip of its smoldering nose to the end of its spiked tail.

6

TORK DARTED out of range just as the first blast of flame blazed down at the polished surface of the proving ground. He felt the heat of it on his back, though the fire itself didn't scorch him.

RAAAAHHHHH! AYEEEEKKK!

Looking back as he ran for his life, he saw Angar charge at the dragon as it swept past. With a howl of rage, he swung his battle axe back, then heaved it forward over his head and let go. The axe spun up toward the beast's underside, blade over handle, unerringly striking its moving target.

And bounced right off with a jarring *clang*. The dragon's tough hide deflected it as if it were no more than a toothpick.

The Southern Horde segment of the audience cried out with dismay as the axe clattered and slid across the field. Their cries were overshadowed by the raucous cheers of the Eastern Horde, however, as Angar made a move of his own.

The dragon looped upward and down again, diving toward the field. Just as it skimmed the bottom of its loop before leaping back up, Angar sprinted under it and swung his mace at a gap between the scales of its tail. The mace's spiky head caught in the gap and held.

As the dragon cruised back into the heights, Angar held fast to the wedged mace. From there, he swung himself around and locked his grip on the upper side of the tail, where he proceeded to climb toward the body proper.

Grimly, he pulled himself hand-over-hand along the tail, trying to ignore the scenery spinning past far below. He made good progress, reaching the central body--only to slip and end up holding on for dear life when the creature suddenly thrashed and changed direction.

Angar regained his grip when the dragon leveled out and resumed his climb. He had almost made it to the base of the neck when another sudden change sent him skidding over the back of the thing. He managed to catch hold of an open orifice, like a gill, only to be shaken all the way clear when the dragon again swooped low.

Angar was pitched from the back of the beast, bounced off one of its wings, and hit the field, where he tumbled to a stop. Meanwhile, his Southern Horde supporters howled encouragement, trying to goad him into boarding the creature again.

As Angar got to his feet, Tork raced in with another attack. Broadsword held high, he charged at the dragon as it dipped over the field, nostrils churning out gouts of flame.

RAAAAHHHHH! AYEEEEKKK!

Swerving on the run, Tork dodged the searing blast and kept up his pace. Just before the beast could launch upward again, he leaped with sword outstretched, its point aimed dead-on at one of the monster's six eyes.

The shot never penetrated, however. At the last second, a gleaming black lid closed over the eye and deflected the weapon, shunting its bearer aside with no effort.

This time, it was Tork's turn to tumble over the field. His supporters howled with disappointment.

It was then that Tork realized the contest might be unwinnable. If even a battle-tested broadsword, battle axe, or mace couldn't make a dent in that dragon, perhaps *nothing* could.

Or maybe *multiple* weapons used by more than one fighter could do the trick.

Tork looked in Angar's direction, wondering if the two of them working together might stand a chance. Could he even talk Angar into it? If he did, would it ruin the contest? Would they both forfeit the ultimate weapon promised by the Blacksmith?

At the rate they were going, simple survival might be the best they could hope for in the end.

The dragon dove and sprayed the field with blistering flame, targeting Angar. As Angar ran a serpentine path across the field, the fiery jet continued to close in, casting up flumes of smoke and steam.

Heart pounding, Tork impulsively took action. Drawing his broadsword, he ran full-tilt toward the front of the dragon. Since the creature was following Angar's zig-zag path, and Tork came in at an angle, he was able to get close without being noticed.

The crowd, however, saw what he was doing and went wild. The cheers from either side of the field were deafening.

The noise might have helped, because Tork was able to get even closer, right under the creature's nose. He waited for a break in the commotion, then screamed at the top of his lungs.

The dragon swung its head around and fixed him in its gaze. Before it could unleash a blast of flame, however, Tork swung back his sword and hurled it like a spear, putting every iota of strength into the throw.

A lifetime of practice and battle paid off, guiding the sword directly into the dragon's left nostril. Tork held his breath, hoping the interior of the nostril was less invincible than the creature's hide, and the blade might do some damage. Perhaps it would even punch straight through to the brain and bring the beast down. Maybe the contest wasn't unwinnable after all.

At least, that was what he hoped until the sword shot right back out and nearly cut him in two. He dove out of the way, barely avoiding certain death--but didn't buy himself much time.

RAAAAHHHHH! AYEEEEKKK!

The dragon's nostrils flared with fiery light as it thrashed its head and took aim. Tork scrambled to get out of the way, even as he knew he was about to be fried alive.

He should have known better, he thought, than to try working in even a limited way with his greatest enemy in all the world.

7

LOOKING BACK OVER HIS SHOULDER, Angar realized he was about to win.

His archenemy had taken Angar's place in the line of fire and was seconds from being incinerated. All Angar had to do was wait, and the man he hated more than anyone would be turned into a sizzling puddle.

Knowing it was coming made Angar feel great relief. After all the years and all the battles between them, he could finally let go and move on. He could live *his* life without it being constantly darkened by the shadow of his nemesis. The new beginning he'd been longing for was finally within reach.

So why did he feel the sick compulsion to get involved?

It made no *sense*. He *hated* Tork with every fiber of his being. Every night, he dreamed of *slaughtering* him. Every day, he dedicated himself to making that dream come *true*.

Why then, in spite of all that, did he find himself

sprinting back toward the dragon with sword upraised, shouting out a guttural battle cry?

Was it because *he* wanted to be the one who did the killing when it came to Tork? That was what he told himself as the dragon swung around to face him.

"Monster!" Angar shook his blade as if it was any kind of threat to the armored beast. "You will *not* rob me of this *reward!*"

Suddenly, the dragon's glowing nostrils were again directed his way. Twin streams of flame shot toward him, only to miss when he bolted hard to the left.

As the fire blasts traced his course, zeroing in, Angar cut right and then straight, heading for the shadow of the great beast's body. It was the one safe place on or above the whole field.

At least until the dragon reared up and turned itself upside-down. In the space of a heartbeat, its nose flipped over to point directly at Angar, whose hiding place was hidden no longer.

"Go ahead then!" he shouted. "Get it over with, foul beast!"

The crowd roared on both sides, drowning out his words. He shook his sword overhead and bellowed another war cry, as if the foe he faced could be intimidated in any way.

Then, another cry sounded from not far away, and Angar spun. To his surprise, that bastard Tork was hurtling toward him, brandishing his mace overhead.

"No!" Tork hollered at the dragon. "One of us must survive!" He ran over and threw himself in front of Angar. "You can't kill *both* of us, or the contest will be for *nothing.*"

The dragon just hung there, its six fiery eyes staring down at them. If it understood what Tork had said, it gave no sign.

Angar, on the other hand, *definitely* understood...and didn't approve. "Get *away* from me!" he snapped, pushing Tork to one side. "I don't *want* your help!"

The instant Angar shoved Tork, the beast's nostrils flared bright crimson and hissed out plumes of smoke. When Tork moved back in front of him, however, the creature hesitated.

"It's working," said Tork. "There can't be a winner if *both* of us are dead!"

"Then this might be that thing's only *weakness*." Suddenly, Angar seized him from behind, clamping his broadsword against his throat. "And *my* only *chance* of *killing* it."

8

FIRE BURNED through Tork's veins as the cold metal of Angar's blade pressed against his throat. Thinking he could work with his enemy in any way had been a mistake, he realized. Angar was utterly without honor, as he had proven time after time in the past.

"You! Dragon!" shouted Angar. "Submit to me, or this man dies!"

The dragon just hung there, gazing down at them with its unreadable crimson eyes. Did it actually understand a word he was saying? Was such a thing possible for an inhuman beast?

"What are you waiting for?" said Angar. "Do you *want* your masters' contest to *fail?*"

As if in response, the dragon lunged forward. Tork felt Angar's grip weaken just a little...just enough.

He hauled up his right leg and heaved his foot back hard into Angar's shin. Angar's breath hissed out between his teeth, and the pressure of the sword let up a little more.

Tork followed by pumping his skull back into Angar's head as hard as he could. The impact left his own head buzzing, but Angar had it worse; he roared in pain and dropped away from Tork, taking his broadsword with him.

Angar stumbled back, grimacing and shaking his head. Mace in hand, Tork spun and stormed after him, seething with rage. The reality of the contest and the dragon hovering overhead fell aside; all he could think of in that moment was bashing his enemy's head in, ending his treachery once and for all.

The howls of the crowd filled the air, but Tork didn't hear them. The blood rushing in his ears overwhelmed all other sound.

He swung up the mace, ready to bring it crashing down with all his strength. Angar was swinging his sword around to stop it, but he was a beat too slow.

Tork gritted his teeth and grinned savagely. So what if he didn't win the Blacksmith's contest? Killing his greatest enemy would be the sweetest reward he could imagine.

Or would it? Just as Tork started his down-swing, the mace was wrenched from his grasp.

He stumbled and nearly fell, lurching around to see what had taken his weapon. Looking up, he saw the handle sticking out of a jagged maw on the dragon's snout. As he watched, it was quickly sucked all the way inside.

Just as the mace disappeared, Angar's sword swept down alongside him, missing his shoulder by a hairsbreadth. Furious, Tork whipped around and kicked the sword from Angar's hand, then lunged at him.

"No more!" shouted Tork, pounding away at Angar with his fists. "Kill you! I'll kill you! I'll *kill* you!"

Cursing like a maniac, Angar fought back with blows of his own. "Die! Die! *Die!*" Then he plowed forward, tackling Tork on the hard surface of the field.

They rolled and wrestled there, fighting with feverish intensity. Soaked with blood and sweat, they struggled to end their long war on the spot--so caught up in the battle between them, they no longer cared about the contest they'd come to compete in.

Then, suddenly, a bolt of sizzling energy struck them both, violently flinging them apart.

"ENOUGH!" The yellow-flamed Blacksmith drifted overhead, glaring down at them. "YOU HAVE BOTH FAILED! YOU HAVE BOTH FORFEITED YOUR PRIZE!"

The crowd, so raucous until now, fell silent.

"No...wait!" Heaving for breath, Tork forced himself to sit up. "Please! There was...no way...to *win.*"

"It wasn't *fair!*" snapped Angar.

"SPOKEN LIKE TRUE FAILURES," said the Blacksmith. "NOW *NEITHER* OF YOU WILL GET THE REWARD YOU DESIRE, AND *BOTH* OF YOU WILL PAY THE PRICE FOR BREAKING THE *RULE* AGAINST *HARMING* EACH OTHER."

"No, please!" Tork scrambled to his feet. "Give us...another chance!"

The Blacksmith's features blurred as he glowed brighter and rotated, throwing off sparks. "YOUR

PEOPLE WILL PAY THE PRICE, AS WELL. THE DRAGON WILL BE UNLEASHED UPON THEM AS PROMISED."

The crowd howled with rage and dismay. It didn't take long for the Eastern and Southern Hordes to run for their camps.

"Don't you *dare!*" Angar leaped at the Blacksmith but couldn't reach him.

"YOU HAD YOUR CHANCE," said the Blacksmith. "NOW YOUR WAR IS AT AN END, AND THIS IS WHAT IT HAS BROUGHT YOU."

All the Blacksmiths spun, and the ground rumbled. The people of the hordes fled screaming, abandoning their warlords on the field.

The dragon slid closer to Tork and Angar, its eyes and nostrils glowing brighter. The two men backed away, looking for a weapon or a way out--finding neither.

Tork swallowed hard and got ready to run, hoping the beast would go after Angar instead. Maybe, just maybe, he would have the lead he needed to elude the creature.

The dragon reared up, and both men bolted in opposite directions. Desperate to survive, unencumbered by the weight of weapons, they ran full-tilt, sprinting like rabbits from a wolf.

But as fast as they ran, it made no difference. The dragon swooped after Angar and scooped him up in its jagged maw, then banked and soared off after Tork.

Tork cleared the field and made for some nearby boulders, hoping they might provide cover. If he could just make it a little further before the flying monstrosity caught up, he might live to fight another day.

Almost there! Almost there! Tork ran harder than ever, pushing himself to reach the boulders before the beast caught up. Maybe, with Angar gone, he could even rally the hordes under his leadership and fight back against the Blacksmiths. Anything was possible, if he wanted it enough.

Until it wasn't.

He was just short of the boulders when he heard the dragon closing in and felt the wind from its wings on his back. He didn't turn and look, just kept running, just kept pushing himself to *survive.*

Maybe that was for the best, as he didn't have to see the dragon's maw open wide and plunge toward him. He didn't have to see it just before it snapped him up like a bird snapping a bug from the surface of a pool.

All he had to see after that was darkness.

PART II

ANGELS ABOVE

9

WHEN TORK OPENED HIS EYES, the first thing he saw was the face of the yellow-flamed Blacksmith--only it wasn't on fire this time. His eyes were bright blue instead of fiery red, his hair was brown with a touch of gray at the temples, and his skin was pale pink instead of bronze.

Instead of robes of flame, he wore a black, long-sleeved uniform with a diagonal stripe running from his left shoulder to his hip. The stripe glowed with blue light, pulsing softly like the beat of a heart—a feature unlike anything Tork had ever seen on the body of a Blacksmith before.

The Blacksmith's voice was different, too--without an echo and not so loud. He spoke in a language that sounded like gibberish to Tork, like nothing he'd ever heard before.

Tork frowned, but then he realized the Blacksmith was talking to someone else. Another face slid into view over the metallic gray ceiling in the background--the face of a middle-aged woman with short black hair and green eyes. Tork thought she looked familiar, but he couldn't place her. Like the other Blacksmith, she wore a black uniform, though the stripe on hers glowed gold instead of red.

The woman spoke to the Blacksmith in the same gibberish he'd used. Her eyes narrowed as she gazed intently down at Tork, studying him.

Confused, Tork tried to sit up...and couldn't move a muscle from the neck down. He could feel his arms and legs and trunk, but they were all paralyzed, locked into place.

Panic swelled in his chest, and his mind raced. The last thing he remembered was being devoured by the dragon. Was he *dead* now? Was this what the afterworld was like?

If so, it wasn't at all like the stories. If he were dead, he should have taken his place in the Never-Ending War, fighting legions of demonic warriors side by side with his glorious ancestors.

Instead, he was *helpless*. Had the Blacksmiths somehow hijacked him from his journey to the Never-Ending War? If so, what plan did they have for him? What would they do to him next?

"Where *am* I?" He scowled up at them, wishing he could break free of their spell. "What have you *done* to me?"

The man and woman continued their stares and gibberish, giving no sign they understood him.

"Am I *dead?* What about my people? You Blacksmiths said you'd unleash the *dragon* on them!"

Still, there was only gibberish from the man and woman.

"I am *lord* of the *Eastern Horde!* If you value your *lives*, I insist you *release* me!"

Still, they did not acknowledge him. The woman said something and the man nodded, apparently talking *about* him but not at all *to* him.

"*Free me!*" shouted Tork. "I demand my *freedom!*"

Just then, there was gibberish from a third voice he didn't know. The man and woman looked away from Tork at someone he couldn't see, and then they moved out of his line of sight.

Seconds after they left, a new face lunged into view, startling him. For one thing, it was much closer; for another, it wasn't like anything remotely *human*. He only knew it was a face because a male-sounding voice was coming from it, speaking the same gibberish as the man and woman.

The face was like a flower in bloom, surrounded by scalloped indigo petals mottled and flecked with white like stars in the night sky. A velvety black nozzle squirmed in the center, pinched into a six-sided star rimmed with white at the end. It was surrounded by twelve twitching purple tendrils capped with glistening yellow beads that might have been eyes.

As for the thing's body, it consisted of thick green stalks wrapped and twisted into roughly the shape of a human form. It was draped with a black uniform like that worn by the human people, but the stripe across its torso glowed with white light, not blue or red.

Confronted with this strange sight, Tork fell silent. He watched as the flower-thing spoke, its black nozzle flexing as the pinched white tip shaped sounds he didn't understand. Like a flower, it gave off a sweet fragrance--though it was *too* sweet and strong and made Tork want to gag.

Perhaps, he thought, this was some weird creature of the afterworld, maybe even a demonic warrior come to recruit him for the Never-Ending War. Whatever it was, it made chills run up and down his spine as it hovered so close to his face, its bizarre mouth parts and beaded tendrils squirming.

Finally, the flower-thing slid away with a rustle of its emerald green stalk of a body, leaving Tork staring up at the empty ceiling. Not seeing the thing made it worse, since he still heard it talking to the man and woman nearby and worried it might do something to him at any moment.

Sweat beaded on Tork's forehead and ran down the sides of his face. Gritting his teeth, he focused all his willpower on regaining control of his body. If he could just *move* again, he could wreak bloody havoc in that place and fight his way to some kind of safety.

As hard as he tried, though, he couldn't break free. His body stayed frozen in place, as useless as a stone in the mud. He was deadlocked.

Then, suddenly, his upper body rose from the hard surface on which he lay, moving to a sitting position. It happened through no effort of his own; he'd done nothing to make it happen. Something had *made* him move against his will.

It was then he got a look at himself and realized his clothes had been changed. The leather harness, straps, scabbards, gloves, and boots he'd worn into battle with the dragon were gone. Instead, he wore a plain gray uniform with a black diagonal stripe and some kind of black shoes.

The strangers had stripped and re-clothed his body. He wasn't prone to shame, but the thought of it infuriated him.

Sitting up, he also finally had a view of the room around him. Looking around, he saw the room was small and simple, little more than four gray walls. The man, woman, and flower-thing stood nearby, staring at him and speaking their usual gibberish.

The woman held some kind of rectangular silver board that blinked with colored lights as she touched different parts of it. Tork realized it was magic when she pressed a green circle on its surface and he found himself moving again.

As the woman touched more parts of the board, Tork pushed himself off the table and stood before her, his feet sinking into the soft black shoes he now wore. Again, every movement was completely involuntary, as if he were watching a complete stranger do it.

Again, the male Blacksmith spoke--but this time, finally, he used words Tork recognized.

"Welcome, Horde Lord Tork," said the man. "You are in a strange new place now. Rest assured, you have nothing to fear."

"I *never* fear *anything*," snapped Tork.

"Perfect," said the woman. "That is one of the reasons we brought you here."

"Where is *here?*"

"Your new home," said the man. "For a little while, at least."

"This is *not* my home!" Tork tried to take control of his body and lash out but could not. He had no more command of his muscles while standing than when he'd been lying on the table. "My home is with my *horde,* and your dragon probably *killed* them all by now."

"The dragon didn't kill them," said the man. "You have my word on that."

"Your word means *nothing* to me!" said Tork. "*None* of this means anything to me!"

"I know this is a lot to take in." The man cleared his throat and stepped forward, away from the other two. "I'll start by introducing myself, though the truth is, we've already met. I'm more than just a Blacksmith, though. I have a name, and it's Gauge. Finn Gauge." He held out his hand toward Tork.

The woman fiddled with her magic board, and Tork's hand swung up against his will to clasp Gauge's and give it a shake.

"How are you *doing* this?" Tork tried and failed to pull back his hand. "I do not *wish* to move this way!"

"Just making sure you hear us out," said Gauge, "instead of killing us with your bare hands right away."

"Not that you've considered such a thing." The woman looked up slyly, then touched a red circle on her board. Tork's hand let go of Gabe's and fell at his side, limp.

"Kill you now or kill you later." Tork narrowed his eyes and glared at her. "Makes no difference to me."

The woman shared a look with Gauge, then touched her board. Again, Tork found his hand reaching out against his will.

"I hope we can avoid such an outcome," said the

woman, and then she stepped forward and shook his hand. "My name is Isabel Haussmann, by the way. Pleased to meet you, Mr. Tork."

"*Lord* Tork!" he bellowed. "I demand *respect!*"

The flower-thing said something in gibberish, and Isabel and Gauge chuckled. Tork knew they were talking about him, and it made his blood boil.

"Release me!" he howled. "I'll *make* you respect me!"

"Very well." The flower-thing reached for Isabel's board and touched a series of colored lights on its surface. "I am *ready* for you to *make* me respect you now."

For the first time since waking, Tork felt in control of his whole body. Unwilling to waste the opportunity, he instantly leaped into action, charging directly at his captors.

In response, the flower-thing's green central stalk suddenly stretched, launching its head and upper body across the room. Like a giant snake, the flower-thing wrapped himself around Tork, immobilizing him in its grip. He struggled but could not break free.

"Tell me," said the flower-thing. "When does the respect begin? I am waiting."

Tork continued to fight his bonds to no avail. He roared in rage and frustration, but that didn't help either. He even bit down on the rubbery vine trapping him, though his teeth didn't make the slightest indentation.

"Where *is* the respect, Horde Lord Tork?" asked the flower-thing. "Am I *missing* something?"

Tork paused, then redoubled his effort, flexing with every bit of strength he could summon. Again, it made no difference.

If anything, the flower-thing's binding stalk got tighter.

"No. No respect yet," said the flower-thing. "Though you might yet earn it, if you try." His head swung around, his face coming to rest uncomfortably close to Tork's. "In the process of doing so, you might wish to address me...but my birth name, as granted on my homeworld, is utterly unpronounceable to your species. Therefore, if you must call me *anything*, you may call me by my *chosen* name among *these* people." He bobbed his head toward Isabel and Gauge. "That name is *Punji Imbroglio*."

Tork scowled and thrashed in Punji's grip. All he could think about was getting free and wreaking havoc on that flower-faced thing, then doing the same to Gauge and Isabel.

Punji just made a snickering sound with his nozzle. "Fear not, little creature. You will have the battle you crave soon enough." Then, he nodded his flowery head at Isabel, who pressed the red light on her board.

As before, Tork lost all control of his body. Punji unwrapped his stalk, leaving Tork standing stiffly with his shoulders squared and arms at his sides.

"Thank you, Isabel." Punji retracted his body to its original, unstretched form between Gauge and Isabel. "I'm thinking we should proceed to the next step of his orientation?"

Gauge nodded. "Now is as good a time as any."

Isabel played the board with her fingers, and Tork started walking. As before, he couldn't control his movements no matter how hard he tried.

"What are you *doing* to me?" he shouted. "*Explain* yourselves!"

"You ought to be happy," said Punji. "We're taking you to see your friend, Angar."

Tork scowled as a door slid open before him. "*Angar* is still *alive?*"

"Yes he is," said Punji. "And I can't *wait* to see the look on *his* face when he gets a look at *you* not being dead, either."

10

It only *looked* like Tork was upside-down to Angar. That was because Angar was hanging from his ankles when Tork approached, marching stiffly through the trees in the big, domed chamber.

"You!" Angar wished he had control of his body, so he could swing hard from the vines that held him and bash his enemy in the groin or gut. "You deserve to be *dead!*"

"How do you know we *both* aren't dead?" Like Angar, Tork wore a gray uniform with a diagonal black stripe across the torso and low black shoes instead of knee-high leather boots.

Angar snorted, his long black hair hanging down around his head as he turned in a slow circle. "Death is no *match* for the great *Lord* of the *Southern Horde!*"

"But *someone* is a match for you, obviously," said Tork. "Otherwise, you wouldn't be *hanging* there instead of trying to *kill* me right now."

Angar ground his teeth and struggled, but still had no

control over his body below the neck. "I'll find a way to do the job, sooner or later. Don't *worry*."

"You want to commit suicide, then?" The flower-man, Punji Imbroglio, stepped out from behind Tork. "Because *that* is what you'll be doing if you ever manage to murder *this* man."

Angar snarled at the sight of Punji, who was the reason he was hanging upside-down in the first place. The plant-man and his friends had awakened him earlier and given him a chance to fight--only to string him up by his ankles when he failed to win the bout.

"You think you'll *kill* me for taking *that* bastard's life?" snapped Angar. "I'd like to see you *try*."

"No, no," said Punji. "That's not *at all* what I'm talking about. I mean you will *literally* die if *he* dies."

"And vice versa," said Isabel as she strolled into view with Gauge. "Your feuding days are over."

Angar and Tork glared at her, then at each other. What she was telling them made no sense.

"It's true," said Gauge. "If either of you dies, the other dies, too."

"At the same time." Isabel snapped her fingers. "Just like that."

"You lie!" shouted Angar.

"Not at all," said Punji. "And there's *more*." His petals and eye-tendrils fluttered, and his whole flower-head swayed on its central stalk. "If you so much as *hurt* each other, you will both be hurt the same way, in equal measure."

"If one causes pain to the other, he will also feel that pain," said Gauge. "It's called *blowback*."

"Welcome to your new reality," said Punji, and he laughed.

"But that isn't *possible!*" Angar was so furious, he felt like his head would explode. "I have never *heard* of such a *curse.*"

"Time for a demonstration." Punji looked at Isabel.

"It's simple. One of you injures the other..." She touched lights on the board, somehow forcing Tork to step forward and thrust a knee into Angar's upside-down belly. "...and *both* of you will experience identical pain."

As the knee sank deep, Angar felt a surge of pain and blew out his breath. He wanted badly to double over, but he couldn't, which just made it worse.

Tork faced the same problem. As the pain he'd inflicted on Angar echoed back into him, he grunted, pinched his eyes shut, and tossed his head from side to side. The cords in his neck tightened, and he looked as if he might topple like a tree...but he couldn't.

"As I said." Isabel worked the board, and Tork stepped back from Angar. "Any pain inflicted on *one* of you will be felt by *both* of you."

"H-how?" huffed Angar. "What kind of *twisted sorcery* is *this?*"

"The kind that keeps you both *alive,* though all you *really* want to do is *kill* each other," said Gauge.

"Remove this spell!" barked Tork. "Do it *now!*"

"Not going to happen." Punji shook his flower roughly for emphasis. "We didn't *bring* you here to *kill* each other."

"Then why *did* you?" snapped Angar. "Why *are* we here?"

"And where *is* here?" said Tork.

"You'll never guess in a million years," Punji said teasingly. "But you'll find out soon enough."

"Suffice it to say, coming here is the most important thing you've ever done," said Gauge. "Your entire *lives* have been leading up to this."

Angar glared. Every minute he hung there away from his horde with the blood rushing into his head, he cared less and less about what his captors had to say. He just wanted to find a way to break free and take out his hostilities on the people who wrongly imagined they could use him without paying the ultimate price.

But he also realized he was still at their mercy. Tackling this problem with brute force was not an option...at least not yet.

"What about my people?" he asked, forcing himself to speak calmly. "The Blacksmiths said they were going to turn the dragon loose on them."

"They're fine," said Gauge. "The dragon was an empty threat, meant to intimidate your hordes. All part of the act, you see."

"What act?" asked Tork.

"The Blacksmiths aren't exactly who we appeared to be," said Gauge. "But theatrics are vital to our mission."

"I don't understand," said Angar. "What exactly are you talking about?"

WOOP WOOP WOOP WOOP WOOP

Suddenly, a deafening noise started blaring, and the light in the chamber changed from white to red. Gauge, Isabel, and Punji were suddenly agitated, looking around nervously.

"What's happening?" Tork shouted over the noise.

There was a loud boom, as if something heavy had crashed nearby, followed by a series of piercing, bestial screeches.

Gauge hollered something in gibberish, and Isabel answered. Punji said something, too, then hurried over to where Angar was hanging.

"Watch your head." Punji popped a long, sharp thorn from his wrist and slashed at the vines holding Angar's ankles. "This could be a bumpy landing."

Angar saw Isabel hit lights on the board, and he felt himself regain control of his body. When the vines gave way, he was able to roll when he hit the ground instead of dropping straight down and breaking his neck.

He sat up just in time to see everyone but Tork dash off into the woods without another word. Whatever was happening, he realized, he and his archenemy were on their own.

And connected so that if one of them was injured or killed, the other one would be, too.

LIKE ANGAR, Tork regained control over his body just as Gauge, Isabel, and Punji ran off into the greenery. He instantly felt a wave of relief as he stretched the muscles in his arms, legs, neck, and back--but it didn't last. With all the noise and red light, he knew he couldn't relax for long.

Though he didn't know exactly what was happening, he knew it couldn't be good.

Fortunately, life as a barbarian in a world of constant peril had prepared him well for dangerous surprises. Already, his mind was racing ahead, considering options for self-defense and evasion, as well as ways to turn the hazards in his favor.

He had a lot of extra thinking capacity now that he wasn't so obsessed with killing Angar--for the moment, anyway.

And he was going to need it.

Somewhere not far away, there was another boom, followed by more bestial screeches. Then there was another boom, and another, and more after that--all spaced precisely apart with a regularity of rhythm that reminded Tork of one thing.

"*Footsteps.*" He said it aloud as Angar drew up beside him. "Something's coming this way. Something *big.*"

"Good." Angar cracked his knuckles. "I spent so much time *frozen*, I'm *dying* to stretch my muscles."

"But we don't know anything *about* this fight," said Tork. "Or this *place,* or these *people.* Maybe it would be better to *avoid* that thing, whatever it is."

"Do what you want," said Angar. "I'll let you know how it works out."

The footsteps got closer, and Angar plunged into the forest after them. That left Tork standing alone, wondering what the best course of action might be...for all of ten seconds. Then he decided it would be better to follow Angar's lead, just in case something bad happened to Angar--and therefore, because of their connection, to *him.*

Charging through the woods in the red light after Angar, he heard the booming footsteps getting ever closer--and then a roar like nothing he'd ever heard before. His heart pounded, and his veins burned with excitement at the prospect of facing whatever menace lurked out of his eyeshot.

Then, when he pushed between trees into a clearing, he finally got a look at it...and stopped in his tracks.

What looked like a giant black insect towered over the clearing, at least three times the height of Tork or Angar. The giant bug stood on four spiny legs and thrashed six clawed arms in the air in a threatening way, roaring to the red-stained heavens.

If there was any doubt of its intentions, it was quickly swept away. The bug slashed one long arm toward Angar, aiming at his neck--only missing, and barely at that, because he suddenly bucked out of the way.

The bug and Angar both roared their fury at the same time, then lunged at each other with unrestrained savagery.

Recognizing that he needed an edge badly, Tork looked around hastily for something he could use as a weapon. The best he could find was a low-hanging tree branch the length of a spear, which he snapped off with a mighty wrench of his arms.

Meanwhile, the giant bug seized Angar in its pincers and hoisted him off the ground. Angar thrashed and fought, to no avail; the bug shook him repeatedly, knocking the wind out of him again and again.

Tork felt every shake through the link, though the bug hadn't laid a claw on him yet. Waves of dizziness washed through him, and his stomach churned as if it were about to empty. One time, the shaking was so extreme, Tork had to drop to one knee to fight off its effects.

If he was going to save himself and Angar, he had to do it soon, or it would be too late.

Springing to his feet, Tork braced the branch spear against his side and charged. The bug looked down but not in time. Before the beast could retaliate, Tork was upon it, driving the jagged tip deep between the chitinous plates on its leg.

Howling, the bug flung Angar aside and reached down

to pluck out the spear. Tork reeled from the sympathetic pain of Angar's fall but still beat the creature to the punch. Yanking the spear free, he whirled to stab it into the joint between the jaws of the insect's clacking pincer.

Again, the bug cried out, its shriek loud enough to carry over the deafening whooping noise that continued to blare all around. It shook the spear free and swept a pincer in Tork's direction, sending him tumbling over the ground and into the trunk of a tree.

As Tork fought to clear his head and regain his footing, the great bug stormed toward him. It reared up, roaring, about to tear him to shreds.

But before it could, Angar scrambled up its back with Tork's spear in hand. Moving fast, he made it all the way to the base of the thing's head and drove it in there with all his strength, drawing gushers of black ichor that sprayed everywhere.

The beast unleashed its loudest shriek of all and dropped heavily to the ground. Angar held on tight to the knobs on its spine and rode it all the way down, stepping off after it slammed into the hard-packed dirt.

Sneering, Angar sauntered over as if he and Tork hadn't been in a life-or-death struggle just now. "I *hate* bugs, don't you?"

Tork gaped at the beast on the ground, its inky blood soaking into the dirt at his feet. Stranger than that, though, were the silvery strands and coils of what looked like metal jutting out of its wounds. Shiny silver shards littered the ground around those openings. "I've never seen a bug like *that* before. Where *are* we, anyhow?"

The blaring whoops suddenly stopped, leaving Angar

in mid-shout as he hollered over them. "Some kind of *hell*, if you ask me. Where *else* would we see monstrosities like *this?*" He kicked the bug hard in the face, but it wouldn't stop twitching.

"The *big* question is, are there *more* of them?" said Tork.

"Not at the moment." Punji's voice piped up unexpectedly, and he stepped out of the nearby brush. "But *trust* me, there are many more like them--and much *worse*--in your immediate future."

"What the *hell?*" Angar scowled. "What's going *on* here?"

"Didn't you run away with the others?" asked Tork. "To escape that *bug* monster?"

"We *did* go elsewhere," said Isabel as she, too, emerged from the brush. "But it wasn't to escape."

"We needed to give you two some *alone time,*" said Gauge, who emerged after Isabel. "So we could see how well you *work together.*"

"Which, let's face it, has not exactly been your *strong suit.*" Punji laughed.

"Wait." Tork frowned at the dead bug. "You mean all this was some kind of *killing test?*"

"No killing, since that was a *mechanical* thing. A *machine.*" Gauge nudged some metallic bits on the ground with the toe of his shoe. "But yes, it *was* a test."

"There *is* a reason we brought you here," said Isabel.

"Which has *nothing* to do with your sparkling *conversation skills,*" added Punji.

"What reason is that?" Angar asked darkly.

"To save your world," said Gauge. "To save *all* of them, actually."

Angar shook his head slowly. "You make it sound like *our* world is not the *only* world."

Punji made a sound like a sigh. "I guess it's time for *the talk*, isn't it?"

"We've put it off long enough," said Isabel.

Gauge nodded. "Come on, then." He walked off, gesturing for Tork and Angar to follow. "Prepare for the Great Revelation."

Tork and Angar hesitated, lagging behind.

"Don't worry," said Gauge. "It won't hurt a bit."

"REMEMBER, there is no shame in being afraid." That was what Gauge said as he led Angar and Tork down the hall. "When the unknown becomes known, it can be a powerful kind of magic."

Angar hunched his shoulders and glowered at the words. The talk of fear made him want to bash Gauge's head in--but as usual, he could not. Though Isabel had allowed him and Tork to have control over most of their movements, they still couldn't lash out at their hosts. He knew because he'd tried several times without success to take a swing at his *least* favorite captor, Punji.

So for now, there was nothing to do but follow along and see what Gauge and the others were talking about.

"So what is this 'Great Revelation' of yours?" asked Tork. "You seemed to be saying it's related to saving the world."

"In a way, yes." Gauge glanced back over his shoulder. "You're about to find out."

He continued to lead them down a gray-walled hallway that looked as if it had been cut from some kind of metal. The hallway curved gently instead of running straight from point to point, for reasons that escaped Angar completely.

Finally, Gauge stopped in the middle of the hall and turned. "Here we are." Walking to the wall, he reached for a panel of colorful buttons mounted there. "You are about to see something you have never before seen in your entire lives...something you have never even *imagined*."

Angar acted calm, as if he didn't care what Gauge was saying--but in truth, he was worried. He knew he was out of his depth, with limited control over even his own *body*. Whatever was about to be revealed, it might make his situation even worse.

"Here we go." Gauge pressed a green button and stepped back to stand beside Angar, facing the wall. "The Great Revelation."

There was a rumble, and the wall began to move. The gray metal slowly slid away like a sleeve from an arm, revealing what at first was a very familiar sight.

It was something he saw every time there was a clear night--a black sky filled with twinkling stars. The only difference was, they looked brighter than usual, and the blackness between them looked darker.

But soon, he saw there was an even greater difference. As the wall continued to slide away, a blue curve appeared, glistening against the darkness. The curve kept growing as the wall moved onward, expanding to a half-circle that revealed more colors and details. Streamers of white swirled over sapphire blue and crinkled blotches of grayish-brown and green.

When the wall cleared the object, Angar saw it was more than a half-circle--it was a *full* one. It hung suspended over the starry black, outlined in bright, golden light.

When the wall was well past the object, it stopped moving. Gauge stepped forward and tapped his finger on the clear barrier left behind it, between the star-filled sky and the mystery place where Angar and Tork now stood.

"Do you know what *that* is?" asked Gauge. "The big *round* thing?"

Frowning, Tork stepped closer. "A hole in the sky?"

"Not even close," said Gauge.

Angar narrowed his eyes and tipped his head to one side, judging. "The painted shield of one of the gods?"

"Nope." Gauge pointed again, more emphatically. "*That* is your *world.*"

Angar said nothing. Gauge might as well have told him it was the back of a turtle, for all the sense it made.

"*This* is what it looks like from a *distance,*" explained Gauge. "A huge *sphere*--a *ball*, hanging in *space.*"

"Space?" said Tork.

"What you see when you look up at the sky at night," said Gauge. "Darkness and stars. Every one of those stars is like your own *sun*, much farther away. And around most of those stars are other *worlds* like yours--other *balls* of dirt, spinning through the night."

"Huh," said Tork.

"Is that so?" said Angar.

"Absolutely." Grinning, Gauge pointed again at the

round object. "That is *your* home, and there are *billions* more just like it out in the vastness of space."

"Balls," said Angar.

"Billions of them," said Tork.

"In space," said Angar.

"Exactly." Gauge nodded.

"Right." Slowly, Angar turned from the view and found Tork was doing exactly the same thing. Their gazes met for a moment by the blue-green glow of the object.

And even though they had spent their lives trying to kill each other, they burst into laughter at the same time.

"Ah." Gauge grinned wider. "Right on time."

"On *time?*" Angar laughed harder than ever. "For *what?*"

"A nervous reaction to an utterly unbelievable situation," said Gauge. "Perfectly understandable and predictable."

"We'd be worried if you *didn't* laugh your asses off at all this," said Punji.

Gauge motioned for Isabel to come closer. "Let's not prolong this," he told her. "Go ahead and show them."

Isabel responded by rapidly working controls on her board. She hit a series of different-colored lights in quick succession, then hit one last light with a flourish, flicking her finger into the air.

It was then that Angar and Tork stopped laughing. There was nothing funny about suddenly flying into space and hurtling pell-mell toward the blue-green world hanging before them.

13

TORK SCREAMED his lungs out as he flashed toward the world, racing along so fast that the stars became blurred streaks around him.

He heard Angar screaming, too, alongside him, but didn't dare look in his direction. He was too transfixed and horrified by the scenery whipping toward him at breakneck speed.

Powerless to slow his flight, he could only watch and wonder where it would stop. All other thoughts were driven from his mind as he rocketed onward and the world grew larger before him.

In seconds, it loomed over him, blocking out everything else in his field of vision. Still, he and Angar blasted forward, zooming through cottony clouds and breaking through into wide-open sky.

They surged downward, soaring past flocks of birds and mountaintops, streaking toward the patchwork of distant fields and rivers. One last burst of speed, and they whizzed through the remaining heights at a heart-stopping pace, swooping ever downward like lightning bolts.

Finally, they slammed to a stop some distance from the ground--too far away to touch it, but close enough to see it was clearly recognizable. Tork knew the place well, having spent so much time through the years riding and hunting and fighting in those rolling green hills. Every bit of it was like an extension of his soul, calling to him from afar.

He hung there a moment, taking it all in, longing to return to it--and then it suddenly flew away from him. Without warning, he and Angar shot back up through the sky, through the clouds, between the stars...and back to the gray hallway where their journey had begun.

When the trip ended, Tork nearly fell over from the shock of it all. He caught himself on the wall and leaned there a while, shivering and gasping for breath.

And the whole time, one realization loomed large in his mind, displacing every other thought and word that tried to occur to him.

That *was* his world out there.

"Take some deep breaths." Gauge was watching Tork and Angar with concern. "You'll both be fine."

"So what did you think?" Punji rustled his petals excitedly. "Not *laughing* anymore, are you?"

"What kind of *sorcery*...?" Angar stumbled, leaned back against the transparent barrier--then hastily pushed away as if it had stung him. "You sent us all the way *down there*...and *back?*"

"Not physically...but yes," said Isabel. "You experienced the true span of *here* to *there*."

"*Here* isn't *there?*" asked Tork. "You mean we're *not* in the *world* anymore? *Our* world?"

"Just so," said Gauge. "In point of fact, you are aboard a *vessel* in *orbit* around your world. A *ship* in *space.*"

"A *magic* ship?" Angar snorted. "You expect us to *believe* that?"

"You can believe whatever you *like*," Punji said off-handedly. "But this is the *truth*, as you have seen. You are sailing on a ship called the *Hellcyon* that is drifting through *space.*"

Angar sneered. "As if *any* ship could *ever* float in space."

"But this one *has*, and it *is,* and it *will* do so again," said Punji. "All thanks to the fantastic power of *science.*"

Tork, who'd never heard that word before, frowned. Based on the magic he'd seen from those people so far, they might just be the greatest sorcerers he'd ever met. "Why is this *sci-ence* so new to us?"

"Because they've been keeping it to *themselves*, obvious-ly," snapped Angar.

"Not true." Gauge shook his head. "Science has been with you always, though you haven't *recognized* it until *now.*"

"If your science is so *powerful*, then *use* it." Angar pointed at the blue-green world. "Send us *back* there. Send us *home*, where we belong."

"That's not going to happen," said Isabel. "You can't *save* your world from *down there.*"

"If *you're* so powerful, why can't you save it *yourselves?*" asked Tork. "Use your *sci-ence* and leave us *out* of it."

"Because science isn't enough." Gauge hit a button on the panel, and the wall started sliding back into place over the starry view. "We *need* you. Otherwise, we wouldn't have gone to the trouble of *bringing* you here."

"You need us why?" asked Tork. "What could magicians as mighty as you possibly need from lowly horde lords like us?"

Gauge looked at Isabel and Punji in turn, his expression hardening. "Because," he said grimly. "The absolute savagery of our enemy can only be countered by equal or greater savagery of our own."

"And even that might not be enough," added Isabel.

"Take it from me," said Punji. "My people, the Gog, are among the greatest warriors this galaxy has ever seen, and even *they* could not stand against this foe we face."

"You say 'foe,'" said Tork. "A *single* enemy is that powerful?"

"The *Caul* contains *multitudes,*" Gauge said darkly. "*Death* and *destruction* on a scale you can ever *imagine.*"

"And you will meet them soon enough," said Isabel. "The time until their arrival is short."

Punji nodded. "*Very* short."

"We can only hope that you and your people are up to the challenge of *fighting* them," said Gauge. "If not, then all is lost."

"Our *people?*" snapped Angar. "You mean the *hordes?*"

"You're planning to bring *them* into this?" said Tork.

"Either that, or they will all surely perish," said Gauge. "Isn't it better to give them a fighting chance?"

"It sounds more like a *death sentence,*" said Angar, "if this *Caul* is as unbeatable as you say."

Tork nodded. "If *you* people, with your mighty *science,*

could not stop them, how can *our* people, armed with swords and axes, hope to fight them off?"

"We have a plan," said Gauge. "You'll see."

"You do?" Angar sneered. "And what about *us?*"

Gauge looked stunned. "Excuse me?"

"Do *we* have a *choice* in this matter?" shouted Angar. "Or did you just *assume* we would cower before your *science* and do your *bidding?*"

No one answered. Had they even *considered* his questions before now?

"That's what I thought," Angar said with disgust.

Isabel sighed. "Maybe he has a point."

"It won't *matter* when the *Caul* gets here!" Punji's petals fluttered, and his eye-tendrils squirmed. "They will *surely* annihilate *Earth* just as they've destroyed *my homeworld* and *millions* of others!"

With that, he stormed off down the hall, bumping Angar's shoulder on his way past.

Frowning, Tork watched him go. "What's Earth?" he asked.

"The name of *your* world," said Isabel.

"No, it isn't," said Tork. "I've never heard of 'Earth' in my life."

"Doesn't mean it's not the planet's name," said Isabel.

"There is much history you know nothing about," said Gauge. "I only wish we had more time to teach you."

"How do *you* know this supposed history?" asked Angar.

"Because." Gauge touched the spot on the wall where the blue-green world had once been visible. "Earth is *our* homeworld, too."

Tork and Angar just stared as his words sank in.

"Now come on." Gauge started down the hall, motioning for them to follow. "I'll give you something to hit, if that will make you feel better about this whole thing."

14

THERE HAD BEEN A TIME, many years ago, when Angar and Tork had not been trying to kill each other.

Angar thought of it now, as the two of them fought side-by-side in an arena against three of the giant mechanical bugs. This time, at least, Gauge and Isabel had armed the horde lords, giving them back their broadswords--but these bugs were more aggressive, their hides tougher. Even with two sword-wielding fighters on the attack, they gave no ground.

But Angar knew it was only a matter of time. He was just that good, and so was Tork.

They'd proved it all those years ago, when they'd been surrounded by lightning bears and stabber rats in the Misbegotten Waste. Friends that they were at the age of twelve, they'd wandered the Waste in search of adventure, trying to prove their young manhood--only to stumble into an ambush by those deadly wild creatures.

Back then, their hordes had been one, united during

the Raider Wars. Their families had been united under the same leader, the legendary Scalder Pacious, and the laws had not forbidden them from running together.

But the lightning bears and stabber rats had nearly killed them anyway. Angar and Tork had battled with every iota of strength and skill they possessed, and *still* they had nearly died.

How many times had Angar saved Tork's life that day? How many times had Tork saved Angar? So many that Angar had lost track.

But he still remembered the feeling of fighting side-by-side and back-to-back against overwhelming odds. He still remembered how it felt to crush the enemy without mercy and walk away *alive*, breathing and laughing along-side someone he was glad to call his *friend*.

How many *true* friends had he known since then? Not too damn many, when he got right down to it. Even seen by the light of their murderous feud, his friendship with Tork had been something special.

Now here they were again, fighting together like they had in the old days--and he didn't hate it. He couldn't deny they still made a good team, even after all their bloodthirsty battles...or *because* of them.

But Angar wasn't sure he liked the direction they were headed and the way things were developing for the two of them.

"So what do you think?" he asked Tork as they pitted their swords against the bugs' pincers, back-to-back. "Do you *like* the idea of being a *warrior-slave* to these people we hardly *know?*"

"They're Blacksmiths, aren't they?" said Tork as he

swung his sword mightily, blocking an incoming pincer. "Maybe that's all we need to know."

"But what if they're *lying* to us about everything?"

With a loud grunt, Tork blocked another pincer strike. "After all we've *seen*, do you really think they're *lying?*"

"It could all be *illusions.*" It was Angar's turn to knock back a pincer. "They could make us see *anything* with their *magic,* couldn't they?"

"I don't know." Tork stabbed the exposed joint between the halves of a pincer claw, then drove the point deeper, dislodging silver wires and gears and drawing gushers of indigo fluid. "These metal bug-things seem real enough to me."

"But what if it's all in our minds? The trip back home, all of it. Just like a third-eye vision-quest conjured up by a shaman."

"Then we might *never* know any better," said Tork. "In which case, it won't *matter.*"

"You don't *think* so?"

"We can't take the chance that they might be tricking us," said Tork. "If we *do*, and they're *not*, this *Caul* could destroy our *world.*"

He had a point, though Angar hated to admit it. "But what about dragging our *hordes* into this? If the Caul is as *powerful* as they're telling us..."

"Gauge said they have a plan."

Angar's sword crashed into a pincer, deflecting it with a *clang.* "And you're willing to gamble your people's *lives* on that plan?"

Tork shouted in rage as he battled back an attack from two directions. "Why are you always *like* this?"

"Like what? *Suspicious? Careful?*"

"No *wonder* I've tried to *kill* you so many times over the years!" snapped Tork. "Everything has to be *complicated* with you."

Angar slashed his sword through a gap in the bug's armor, tearing through a good-sized strip of some kind of metallic mesh. "So you're planning to go along with the Blacksmiths' plan, whatever it is? Meaning *I'll* have to do the same, since we're *connected?*"

"You don't *have* to."

"If I want to make sure you don't get *killed* and take me down *with* you, I do." Angar followed his big slash with another through another exposed strip of mesh, getting even better results. The big bug squawked and stumbled back, thrashing its broken appendage as it spurted indigo fluid all over the place.

"True," said Tork. "Or maybe I hate you so much, I'm *willing* to get killed, if it means taking you down with me."

"You'll *never* do that," said Angar. "You're too obsessed with being the last one *standing.*"

Tork paused in his latest swordfight and turned, staring coolly at Angar through narrowed eyes. "Am I?"

Then, with a flourish, he whirled back to the fight, pressing the bug further back with each stinging blow.

Leaving Angar to glare at him, good feelings of the distant past forgotten, before returning to his own savage battle with a towering, robotic insect.

15

Tork stood in the dimly lit hallway, gazing out at the dark circle of his world among the stars.

It was night down there now, with his side of the world facing away from the sun. Crackles of lightning arcing across storm clouds provided the only light visible from the ship.

But he knew there must be campfires on the ground, though he couldn't see them. The flashing of animals' eyes in the darkness...the glow of smokers' pipes packed with burning tobacco...the glinting of sword blades by starlight...all these and more, he knew were down there.

He saw them all when he closed his eyes. That world, his home, was in his head, and always would be for as long as he lived.

If only he could go back there right now in person, he would be happy. Maybe he could even sleep soundly-- something he didn't seem to be able to do on that ship out in space, for some reason.

"Figured out how to open the viewport on your own, did you?" Just then, Gauge strolled up the hall, arms folded across his chest. He wore loose-fitting black clothing and looked sleepy, as if he'd been in bed.

Tork shrugged. "I just had to hit the one button."

"You also figured out how to leave your quarters and find your way here," said Gauge. "The one stretch of corridor you've been cleared to explore."

"It wasn't hard," said Tork. "More buttons."

"Good, good." Gauge nodded. "You're adjusting to technology remarkably quickly."

"I am?"

"One day ago, the concept of a spacecraft was utterly foreign to you. The idea that your *world* was a planetary body spinning through *space* was beyond your understanding. Now look at you." Gauge grinned and patted Tork's shoulder. "We'll make a star warrior of you yet."

Tork looked at him, then returned his gaze to the dark, distant planet. "Earth," he said simply.

"Yes." Gauge pulled his hand away. "The mother world. The cradle of humanity."

"Earth," repeated Tork. "Why have I never heard that name before?"

Gauge clasped his hands behind his back. "So much knowledge was lost," he said grimly. "The slate was wiped almost completely clean. We call this time Age Zero."

Tork frowned. "How did it happen?"

"Wars. Natural disasters. Epidemics." Gauge sighed. "Many things over a long period of time...and then a *longer* time after that of starting *over* from *scratch.*"

"From scratch?"

"With nothing," said Gauge. "The human population almost completely bottomed out. The environment was ruined thanks to pollution, climate change, and nuclear blasts. The few survivors had no access to modern technology, knowledge, or medicine."

"Then how did they survive?"

"Sheer determination," said Gauge, "and a little help from certain *interested parties.*"

Tork did the mental math and nodded. "Like the Blacksmiths."

Gauge nodded. "The Blacksmiths preserved knowledge and resources through Age Zero, keeping it ready for the rebirth of civilization."

"Which is now? We're ready now?"

Gauge shook his head. "Not even close. After two thousand years, humans are still living as barbarians under primitive conditions. We estimate it will be at least another *thousand* before the human race is again ready for anything more civilized."

"Is that what you people think?" asked Angar, who approached from around the bend in the corridor. "We're not *worthy?*"

"That's not it at all," said Gauge.

Angar ignored his answer. "Why are *we* here, then, if we're not *worthy?* If we're not *ready?*"

"Because it doesn't matter anymore," said Gauge. "You're out of *time.* We *all* are."

"The Caul," said Tork.

Gauge sighed. "Everything we've done. The long road back for humanity. *All* of it will be for *nothing.* It probably already *is.*"

"Then why even try?" asked Angar. "Why not just send us home and let us enjoy the time we have left the way we choose?"

"Is that what you want?" Gauge stepped forward and pressed his open hand against the clear wall, framed by the dark orb of the nighttime Earth. "To give up? To let your world die without a *fight?*"

Angar scowled. "I'm just saying..."

"Because that can be easily arranged," snapped Gauge. "We can throw *Earth* to the *wolves* and *move on.*"

"Then *do* it," said Angar. "You have a *ship.* Go find some *other* world to defend."

"It's not that simple." Gauge slumped. "There aren't that many inhabited worlds *left* in this galaxy that aren't under the thumb of the Caul. So many planets and peoples have been subjugated and culled by them." His hand fell away from the wall. "It is a dark time for the cause of freedom in this galaxy."

No one said anything for a long moment. Stars twinkled silently beyond the wall, marking the circular shape of the darkened world.

Finally, Tork cleared his throat and spoke. "You really think *we* and our *people* stand a chance?"

"I *hope* so," said Gauge. "Isn't that enough?"

"Why don't *you* and *your* friends do the fighting?" asked Angar. "You've got the *science*, that's for sure."

"We're trying," said Gauge. "We've banded together with survivors from a score of other worlds and pooled our resources to wage the war. We call ourselves *The Undoing*, because we've pledged to undo the horrors of the Caul. We shall be *their* undoing in the end. At least, that's our intention." His shoulders sagged. "The reality is, the odds are very much against us. As a group, we lack the one thing that gives the Caul their greatest power."

"What's that?" asked Tork.

"It's the single quality that above all others that has enabled humanity to survive against incredible odds." Gauge turned and raised a clenched fist. "*Savagery.*"

"You don't have it?" asked Tork.

"Not the way that you do," said Gauge. "We've bred it out of ourselves to prevent another *apocalypse* like that which set Age Zero in motion. Many of the other species in The Undoing lack it as well, for one reason or another. Now we realize that we need it more than ever."

Angar smirked. "You need the will to *slaughter.*"

"To do anything, no matter how awful, in order to survive," said Gauge.

"I don't know." Angar shrugged. "The way you've treated *us,* you might be better at it than you give yourselves *credit* for."

Just then, there was a sharp pinging sound in the hall. It stopped when Gauge tapped the lobe outside the canal of his right ear. Tork had seen the gesture before and knew someone was talking to him, someone Tork couldn't hear.

"Yes?" Gauge listened for a moment. "I see. How long do we have?" Whatever he heard next, his face turned ashen gray. "I understand."

With that, he tapped his earlobe again and turned his full attention back to Tork and Angar. "The situation has changed," he said grimly. "You'll get to fight sooner than we thought."

"It's just as well." Angar glared at him. "I'm in the mood to *kill* something right now."

"You won't have much time to prepare," said Gauge. "To train with the weapons. To learn what you need to know."

Tork shrugged. "The sooner the better. Tell me what to kill, and I will kill it."

"It's not that simple. It's not like fighting on Earth, at home."

"What's the worst that can happen?" Angar laughed. "One of us gets *killed* and takes the other down *with* him?"

"No, actually." Gauge looked gravely serious. "It can be *much* worse than that."

Tork laughed, too. "Worse than getting killed?"

"You'll see," said Gauge. "You'll find out. And then you'll wish you hadn't."

Angar shook his head and patted Gauge on the back. "The Caul will be the ones wishing they hadn't met *us.*"

"I'm sorry you said that." Gauge shook his head.

"I'm never sorry about *anything,*" snapped Angar.

"Because you've never met the *Caul.*" Gauge checked a device on his wrist and let out a sigh. "But you have a *little* time until then to enjoy your innocence."

"*Innocence?*" Tork laughed hard. "*Him?*"

Gauge ignored the remark. "We have a great deal to do in that very limited time. Now come with me."

"Wait." Angar blocked his way. "We've talked a lot about what *we're* expected to do for *you.* But you left something out."

Gauge scowled, looking impatient. "What's that?"

Angar stood tall and stared down at him. "What are *you* going to do for *us?*"

For a moment, Gauge just stared back at him. He looked confused, as if the question had never occurred to him before.

Then, he shrugged. "Saving the galaxy. Undoing the atrocities of the Caul. Isn't that enough?"

"What do *you* think?" said Angar. "I didn't even know there *was* a galaxy a day ago."

"Give it time," said Gauge. "Your outlook will change."

"Or maybe *yours* will," said Angar, "when *I* get done with you."

Then, he smiled cruelly and stepped aside. Gauge glared at him for a moment, then marched past, waving for them to follow.

"Let's go," he told them. "It's time to meet the enemy."

As they fell in step behind him, Angar leaned in and whispered to Tork. "I thought maybe we already had."

16

"Brace yourselves," said Gauge as he hurried down the corridor. "The Cortex can be a little overwhelming at first."

"*Nothing* overwhelms *me*," snapped Angar.

"You might be surprised," said Gauge. "You're about to see what might seem to you like some very strange sights."

"Such as?" asked Tork.

"Creatures from other worlds, unlike anything you've seen before on Earth," said Gauge. "The peoples of The Undoing come from all over the galaxy, and representatives of many of them live and work aboard this ship."

Angar chuckled. "No creature under the sun—*any* sun—can *ever* surprise me."

Gauge looked back with a knowing smile. "Don't say I didn't warn you."

Without slowing, then, he veered left and charged toward a door in the wall, which slid open before him.

Tork and Angar kept pace, marching through with confidence as if they'd done it a thousand times before.

Then, the barbarians both stumbled, surprised to see the starry darkness of space under their feet.

They braced themselves as if they thought they might fall into the firmament and drift away...then looked around and realized they stood on a see-through floor like everyone else in the room, and no one but them seemed to take any notice of it.

A huge chamber fanned out around them, wedge-shaped and crowded with distractions. Though the floor and ceiling were transparent, the walls were covered in banks of screens and flashing lights.

Everywhere they looked, people in colorful uniforms scurried over that see-through floor—a mix of men and women of every race Tork and Angar had ever seen, and a few they hadn't. Strange creatures moved among them, including flower people like Punji, shiny red people who looked like they'd been turned inside-out, and furry brown things like grizzly bears but with eight tentacles. There were other things moving about, too, made of crystal or metal or cloud, but neither Tork nor Angar were sure if they were alive or something else altogether.

The place was a jumble of movement and noise, an assault on the senses. There were constant shouts, beeps, whoops, buzzes, and crashes from all directions—things falling, people arguing, machines squawking. Bursts of strange languages and smells swirled and mingled, and weird streams of glowing text and images danced in midair.

The barbarians just stood and took it all in, unsure

what they were seeing, hearing, and smelling. The one thing that did penetrate the understanding gap was the sense of barely controlled chaos in the room; it reminded them both of a horde camp before battle, with everyone scrambling to get ready for a fight.

Gauge waded into the chaos without hesitation, asking rapid-fire questions and watching passing text streams and screens on devices mounted on pedestals in the heart of the room. As soft-spoken as he was, people jumped when he spoke and answered fast, delivering whatever information he'd requested.

Seeing him like that, Tork understood. "He's like us," he told Angar, pointing his chin in Gauge's direction. "He's a Horde Lord."

Angar sniffed. "Then he's the one we have to kill when it's time to take over."

Just then, Gauge looked back and waved for them to join him. Was he oblivious, wondered Tork, or just plain stupid? Did he really think they wouldn't find a way to break free and take his power for their own?

Maybe Gauge and his people didn't *deserve* to survive.

"Welcome to the Cortex." Gauge raised his voice over the noise and spread his arms wide. "Control center of the battleship *Hellcyon*."

"So this is where the orders are given." Angar couldn't resist a satisfied smile as he looked around.

"It seems like an *out-of-control* center to me," said Tork.

"You're right," said Gauge. "We had to launch this ship early, and we're still ironing out some bugs in the systems and procedures. *Now*, we don't even have time for *that*. There's been an incursion."

Tork and Angar both frowned at the word, which the translation system wasn't quite getting across to them.

"The enemy has arrived at our perimeter." Gauge pulled out a silver control board and tapped a series of colored buttons. An image of starry space unfolded in midair, with a large yellow ball of light in the middle, circled by smaller spheres.

Tork narrowed his eyes and leaned in for a closer look. "What is that?"

Suddenly, Punji's squirming black nozzle plunged out of the floating image, making it ripple. "It's the *solar system!* It's where you *live!* I swear, sometimes it's like you've been stuck in the barbaric *dark ages* all your lives." With that, he quickly withdrew, and the image settled.

"Solar system?" said Tork.

Gauge pointed a finger at the big yellow ball in the image. "That's the sun," he said. "What it looks like from a distance. And that..." He pointed at a much smaller, blue-green ball. "...is Earth. And *that*..." He pointed at a much bigger ball, striped with many colors and a giant red spot on its belly. "...is *Jupiter.* On one of its moons, Io, *we* have a station. A *camp*, if you will."

"And it's also where *they* are," said Punji. "A *small* ship. A *scout*, probably."

"But that's enough, when it comes to the Caul." Gauge scowled. "Just *one* of them could wipe out our entire station like *that*." He snapped his fingers. "And summon a Caul fleet to strike Earth."

Angar tried snapping his fingers, too, but couldn't quite figure it out.

Gauge turned to a young woman with dark brown

skin and tightly-braided black hair. "How long will it take us to get there, Lieutenant Jelani?"

Jelani looked flustered as she tapped keys on a control board cradled in the crook of her left arm. A stream of glowing yellow numbers unspooled from thin air before her, and she read them with flicks of her dark green eyes. "A little over two days, if the rippers run right."

"Rippers?" asked Tork.

"Rip engines." Faced with the barbarians, Jelani considered her words carefully. "The machines that push us through space."

"*Rip* it open and throw us through the rip to the other side, to be exact," explained Gauge.

"The fastest engines ever built," added Jelani.

"By the *Caul*." Punji snorted. "We *stole* 'em. And we still don't know if they'll *work* right on this damn ship."

"They'll work." Jelani nodded firmly. "I'd bet my life on it."

"And *our* lives, too," said Punji. "And, by extension, the lives of everyone in the galaxy who's depending on us."

"No sweat." Jelani smiled.

"All right then," said Gauge. "How long until we can launch?"

Jelani checked data streams and readouts, tapping keys on her control board. She shouted something in a different language to one of the tentacled grizzlies, and the grizzly roared something in return.

"Ideally, seven hours," said Jelani. "Or right now, if you want to live dangerously."

Gauge looked wryly at Punji, eyebrows raised. "What do you say?"

Punji flexed his black snout and ruffled his indigo petals. "I say, *Banzai!*"

Gauge shook his head. "This isn't a *suicide mission.*"

"Says you." Punji laughed and twisted his flowery head all the way around, then back.

Gauge turned to the barbarians. "I suggest you hold on to something, gentlemen. The ride could get bumpy."

Angar snorted and squared his shoulders. "A *horde lord* needs only to hold on to his *sword* and his *battle axe.*"

"Suit yourself." Gauge jammed two fingers between his lips and blew out a shrill whistle that pierced the din in the Cortex. Everyone stopped jabbering, hollering, and squawking at once, though the multitude of devices continued to make noise throughout the room. "Listen up, people! It's time!"

Tork and Angar shared a look. Gauge's command of the crew was obvious.

"I don't have to tell you what's riding on this, do I?" As Gauge spoke, he looked around at all the eyes fixed upon him. "We all know why we're here today. We of The Undoing have worked long and hard to make this day a reality. And we all know why *they* are here today." He gestured at Tork and Angar. "*This* is where it all starts! *This* is where we make history!"

Everyone in the Cortex stared at Gauge with laser focus. Most of them nodded at his inspiring words.

"Are we *ready* for this?" he continued. "The truth is, we *have* to be. Our only other choice is inaction, and through inaction, *extinction.*"

People started speaking up in agreement, calling out "No" and "Not that" and "Never."

"*Now* is the time!" said Gauge. "The only time we *have!* Who's *with* me?"

"*One and all!*" Everyone in the Cortex shouted the words at once, pumping arms and tentacles and all manner of strange appendages in the air. "*One and all!*" They said it again and again in perfect unison.

Tork and Angar were the only ones who didn't join the battle cry—though Tork was so moved by the spirit in the room that he mouthed the words silently.

"Prepare for launch!" howled Gauge, and a deafening cheer roared through the Cortex.

Then, everyone burst into action, racing around the room to make last-minute adjustments.

"Start the countdown!" When Gauge said it, a band of yellow light spun into existence around the upper rim of the Cortex, bright red numbers flashing through it—a countdown starting at 10. A mechanical male voice recited the numbers aloud, in time with the countdown.

10...9...8...

As the countdown continued, the crew leaped into seats and couches around the Cortex and quickly secured themselves with straps. Gauge dropped onto a nearby chair, too, and strapped himself in. The sound of dozens of buckles snapping into place rose in counterpoint to the counting of the computerized voice.

7...6...5...

A rumbling sound started from somewhere deep in the ship, shaking the Cortex and everyone in it. A high-pitched whine built along with it, intensifying with each passing second.

4...3...2...

Only Tork and Angar stood on the quaking deck, looking around at the locked-down crew. Tork had a flash of doubt and headed for one of the few unoccupied seats, a chair mounted on the wall.

But Angar just sneered at him with disgust and waited for what was coming.

... 1...zero.

And then it happened.

The ship lurched violently, slamming Angar to the deck. Landing facedown, he saw the space underneath the vessel spin clockwise like a whirlpool, the light of the stars within it stretching and twisting into gossamer white streamers.

Then, the ship lurched again, and crackling bolts of wild blue lightning flashed out of it toward the whirlpool below. When the blue bolts leaped into that spinning swirl, it tore open into a ragged maw suffused with cascading white light.

Grunting, Angar pushed himself up off the floor, straining against the great heaviness that was keeping him pinned. Just as he got to his knees, the ship suddenly plunged, forcing him back down again so hard, he howled in pain.

The *Hellcyon* dropped fast toward the coruscating tear, spinning and tumbling out of control. Stuck to the rumbling deck, ears filled with the deafening whine of the engines, Angar could only watch through his squinting eyes as the rip in space shot closer.

Then, with a final surge of speed, the ship leaped into the rip, engulfed in that searing white light. Everything seemed to stretch to impossible lengths aboard the ship, and Angar let loose a roar of agony and despair as his senses erupted in maddening confusion.

It was only then, as his brain blazed with a jumble of images, sounds, and feelings for which he had no comprehension, that Angar blacked out, dealing with the crazy-quilt input flooding into him from the rip in the only way his overloaded brain possibly could without going insane.

17

"HE'LL BE ALL RIGHT. Just a little case of Rip sickness." The words emerged from the lips of Angar, who was sprawled on the deck of the Cortex, but they weren't his. Tork understood that much.

Barely.

"It's not uncommon, as you know, to experience a negative neurological reaction to the Rip Drive," continued Angar/not-Angar. "To make matters worse, this man has never experienced any form of space travel before."

Gauge, who crouched beside Angar, frowned deeply. "I wish we'd had more time to prepare him better." His eyes flicked over to Tork, who was crouching on the other side of Angar's inert form. "To do *lots* of things, actually."

"I've already begun treating his brain from within," said Angar/not-Angar. "Restoring certain balances and adjusting for trauma. He should be up and around again in a few hours."

"Excellent." Gauge nodded. "Take good care of him, Doc."

"Will do." Angar/not-Angar raised a hand in a thumbs-up gesture. "No sweat, kemosabe."

Tork scowled. He had seen the ghostly form of Dr. Delilah Mode merge with Angar's body. He'd been told she was possessing him, somehow healing him with her magic from the inside out. But he still didn't fully *grasp* the specifics of what was happening or accept that his fellow barbarian would be helped and not harmed.

Though accepting things without grasping them seemed to be his lot in life these days.

"All right then." Gauge got to his feet. "Our other friend here will just have to pick up the slack until he's back in action." He raised his eyebrows at Tork. "That sound fair, Tork? Covering for Angar on the work we planned for the two of you?"

Tork shrugged. "I have no idea."

"Good enough for me." Gauge patted him on the shoulder on the way past. "You'll do fine. This is right in your wheelhouse, my friend."

"Wheel...house?" As Tork said it, he imagined a large, wooden wheel resting alongside a wooden shed like his people's shrine to the death gods back home.

"It's something you're well-qualified for," said Gauge. "You and Angar are better at it than anyone else on the ship, in fact."

"Not *everyone*," said Punji as he trailed after them.

"We can *all* learn a few things from them," said Gauge as he crossed the Cortex. "Every single one of us. But we have to do it fast." The exit door whisked open, and he hurried through it without slowing. "We only have two days until we get to Io, and we'll have to be as ready as we can be by then."

TORK COULD NOT HELP FEELING disgusted as he stood at the front of the big room—the *gymnasium*, Gauge had called it—and surveyed the crowd before him. They were *nothing* like the warriors of the Southern Horde or even the inferior Eastern Horde back home on Earth.

And *he*—and Angar, when he awakened—were expected to turn them into just that, and in a limited time, no less.

At least Tork felt more like his warrior self in the clothes they'd given him—a return to the gear he'd worn daily as Horde Lord. It wasn't *exactly* the same as what he'd been wearing when the Blacksmiths had brought him in, but it was much better than the gray jumpsuit he'd been wearing ever since. He wore a leather harness, breeches, belt, gloves, and boots—so much like his original gear, yet studded with glowing, colored buttons and etched with symbols he didn't understand. The scabbard on his back and the holster at his hip were empty of the weapons that should have been there. Only his headband seemed to be the actual original item he'd once worn, complete with the blood-red jewel in the center on his forehead.

Standing there in that garb, he felt more like himself than he had since leaving home. If only he could close his eyes and wish himself back there, he could escape the task of training those hopeless people in the art of war, which seemed impossible.

After all, they were mostly toothpicks. Of the three dozen or so men and women standing before him in white jumpsuits and rubber-soled white shoes, only a handful had any kind of formidable-looking frame.

And not one of them, from what he could see, had the steely glint of a killer in their eyes, not even a little.

Suddenly, Tork found himself wishing that *he* were the unconscious one instead of Angar.

"Thanks for joining us, Tork." Gauge walked in from the corridor, wearing his own white jumpsuit, and stood beside him. "We need your help getting ready to face the Caul on Io."

Tork looked out at the unimpressive crowd. "Training can only do so much."

"We understand," said Gauge. "But we've been studying video recordings of your technique in our spare time. Everyone in this room has made a commitment to learning what you have to offer."

Tork scowled. "Video recordings?"

"The Blacksmiths have followed your career for many years," explained Gauge. "Though it's true, we thought we'd have more time to follow it further and apply what we've learned."

Tork frowned. What could these people have learned from "video recordings?"

"With more time, none of us would be standing here right now." Gauge swung an arm wide to take in the crowd. "We'd be at our posts, and we'd have an army ready for you to lead into battle."

"An army?" asked Tork.

"The Southern and Eastern Hordes," explained Gauge. "We were planning to bring them along...but we ran out of time. We had to leave Earth orbit much sooner than expected, so *these* are the only fighters we have to offer you." Again, he gestured at the crowd.

Tork's heart sank at the thought that his horde *could* have been there at his back, ready to march with him into whatever challenge lay ahead...and wasn't. If all he had to work with were the people in white jumpsuits slouching before him, he was in terrible trouble.

"What about your *science*?" he asked. "Isn't it mighty enough to crush your enemies?"

Gauge shook his head. "If science alone were enough, the Caul would not have triumphed against so many advanced peoples. They would have been stopped long ago."

How many times had Tork seen desperation in a man's eyes? Now here it was again, glowing in the depths of Gauge's gaze...pushed back as far as it could go but still there, still visible.

As great as the power these people possessed, they faced a threat that could be the end of them all. They needed Tork to help them win the fight.

Though that still didn't change the fact that he didn't have much to work with here.

Grunting, he looked around the room for inspiration but found none. How could he teach these people without *wounding* or *killing* them?

"I don't know where to begin," he said.

Suddenly, the door flew open, and Angar bounded into

the room. "I hear you people need some *war training!*" His lips peeled back in a vicious grin. "Well, it looks like I woke up just in time!"

Sneering, he stormed toward the crowd, which parted to make way for him. Like Tork, he was back in his Horde Lord gear, leather straps straining to contain his hairy bulk.

"Lesson one!" hollered Angar. "The thing you need *most* to crush a *foe!*"

With the speed of a striking viper, he lashed out a massive hand and grabbed the closest person—a scrawny, blond-haired man—by his throat.

"You're about to feel it more than you ever have before!" said Angar. "And it will *feed* you such *power* that even your substandard weakling *bodies* will fight like *behemoths!*"

Jolting the man toward him, Angar spit in his face. Teeth bared, he shook the man like a rag doll, then tossed him to the floor at the feet of an attractive young woman with short, dark hair.

"*Hatred!*" howled Angar. "The craving for *vengeance! This* is what you need! And *I* will be the one to give it to you!"

With that, he leaped into action, mowing down people right and left—shoving them, thumping them, heaving them into each other. The few times someone tried to stand up to him, he treated them with special violence, chucking them through clusters of people like a bowling ball through pins. The whole time, he never stopped laughing uproariously.

And he didn't stop mowing until every last person was sprawled on the floor or atop a pile of other people.

"There!" He dusted off his hands as he walked over to face Tork. "*That's* how you teach *weaklings*. You put the *hatred* in them."

"That's the *opposite* of training," snapped Tork. "Breaking their *bones* won't get them ready to fight!"

"I broke *nothing!*" Angar bared his teeth at Gauge. "Except their *complacency*." He popped forward as if to head-butt Gauge. When Gauge ducked back from the blow that never came, he laughed loudly. "They're better off now! Trust me!"

Then, laughing some more, he strolled out of the gym and into the corridor, Tork and Gauge the only two left standing in his wake.

As the door swooped shut behind him, Gauge sighed and tapped the lobe of his right ear. "Doctor Mode? We need a med team in the gym, stat."

As Tork surveyed the carnage in the room, one question loomed in his mind: *What was Angar trying to accomplish?*

Then, as he turned to Gauge, another question arose, as well. *Why didn't he stop Angar?*

After all, Gauge had already proven he could take control of the barbarians' bodies. Why hadn't he switched off Angar before all those people had gotten hurt?

Or was it possible the Blacksmiths' control wasn't as complete as they'd led their captives to believe?

And Angar was testing the limits to see what he could get away with when the time came for whatever he had in mind.

BEFORE

EARTH, 10 YEARS AGO

THE AMBUSHERS SHOULD HAVE KNOWN BETTER.

They outnumbered Tork and Angar seven to two. They had the element of surprise on their side. They had more weapons and carried shields. They were more experienced than the two young warriors.

And they didn't stand a chance.

Leaping out from behind dirt mounds in the heart of the Misbegotten Waste, they charged the two friends with weapons drawn. They howled a fierce war cry as they rushed toward them, seven brawny killers bound for blood.

And within a handful of minutes, they were dead to a man.

Grinning, long hair flying, Angar and Tork whipped into action. Their gleaming blades smashed aside the swords and clubs and maces of the enemy, blowing through them with powerful strokes. Working in unison, perfectly synchronized, they plowed through the shields, then hacked and sliced and pounded away at their foes.

The enemy's war cries turned to wails of agony. The

clashing of steel turned to the chopping of blades into flesh. Body parts shot through the air, and blood sprayed everywhere.

It was a true dans macabre, a ballet of gore and savagery. At the end, only two men were still standing, their bodies drenched in the blood of fallen foes.

"Nice work." Angar clapped a hand on Tork's shoulder.

Tork nodded and smiled. "You, too."

Their friendship had never been stronger. For as long as they could remember, they'd been friends, growing up together as part of the Grand and Glorious Horde. They'd seen each other through good times and bad, rising now as young men to take their rightful places among the Horde's elite fighters. Even Scalder Pacious, the legendary lord of their horde, showed them respect and rewarded their courage.

Yet even they were not always prepared for what fortune might bring.

As they stood there, congratulating themselves for a fight well won, a sound reached them from one of the mounds where the ambushers had hidden.

It was a muffled, high-pitched voice, a human *voice.*

The two set off without a word, weapons at the ready. They hadn't lived to the age of 17 without surviving many a trap through the years.

Just as they reached the mound, a body rolled out from behind it and came to rest in front of them. Their hearts beat faster at the sight of her, lying on her back in the dirt, wrapped tightly in ropes from shoulders to toes.

A woman. *A young* woman who wasn't from their horde.

Tork ran over, pulled the white cloth gag from her mouth, and she spoke.

"Thank Yorg!" she said. "You got me away from those slavers!"

"It was the least we could do." Angar didn't mention that he and Tork had been the ones attacked by the slavers in the first place. "You're free now."

"Not really." She wriggled in the dirt, demonstrating the bonds wound around her.

Tork and Angar cooperated to quickly unwrap her. As they did, they both noticed the sweet scent that clung to her, a perfume like the fragrance of the sweetest-smelling flower they'd ever known. She didn't smell at all like the horde girls back at camp, rough and unwashed as they almost always were.

By the time Tork and Angar finished, she was kneeling in the dirt with the ropes piled around her, wincing and rubbing her wrists.

"Thank you." Free of the bonds, they could see she was slender and beautiful, her face a soft oval, her hair long and red. A tiny dark mole perched above the left corner of her mouth, and her bright green eyes sparkled in the sunlight. "My name is Lillia. And you?"

Angar pushed forward and slapped his chest with an open hand. "I'm Angar!"

Tork pushed ahead of him and bowed, his long, blond hair falling around his face. "And I'm Tork."

"Listen." Leaning on the mound, she worked her way to her feet. "Is there somewhere you can take me? Somewhere safe? Because trust me, there'll be more of those people coming to take me back."

Tork and Angar exchanged a look as they did the mental math. The pretty girl needed their help. She was practically begging them to take her home with them.

What harm could there be in that?

"Okay," said Tork. "Let's go. We'll take you someplace safe."

"You will?" asked Lillia. "Oh, thank you!"

"My friend and I will protect you," said Angar. "And our lord will know what to do with you."

Lillia looked deeply relieved. "I'm so lucky you found me— two good, strong men like you."

"We know." Angar smirked and jostled Tork with his elbow. "People tell us that all the time."

"TAKE A SEAT, PLEASE." Isabel gestured at the chairs around the long, elliptical table when Angar and Tork walked into the room. "Let's get started."

While Tork dropped onto one of the chairs alongside the table, Angar stomped in and plunked himself down on the glossy black table itself, right at the head. He then proceeded to look around nonchalantly, as if he'd acted with perfect decorum.

"You've trained some of our people." Isabel walked to the far end of the room, carrying her silver control board with the colored-light buttons on it. "Now, it's time for *us* to train *you* a bit."

"We are horde lords," said Angar. "Not *pets* to be *trained.*"

Isabel looked at him blankly. "*Inform*, then. It's time to *inform* you about the mission."

Angar smirked and said nothing.

Isabel cleared her throat, then tapped buttons on the

board. The lights in the room dimmed, and a three-dimensional image of a starfield appeared over the table, hovering in midair.

"This is our solar system." She worked the board, and the familiar image of the big yellow sun orbited by planets zoomed up from the starfield. "Here's our current location." The image zoomed in more, and a glowing red X enclosed in a circle appeared, blinking in the starry space between a small red planet and the giant, striped one with the crimson eye. "And this is where we're headed." A tiny dot near the striped giant started blinking. "Io, moon of the planet Jupiter."

The image zoomed in close on the blinking dot, and it expanded into a pale yellow and white sphere flecked with black and rust. As Tork watched, the sphere turned slowly and revolved around the striped orb of Jupiter.

"The enemy scout landed in the moon's northern region, not far from our station," explained Isabel. "The station sent out a reconnaissance team that went silent and never returned."

"Recona...conasun..." Angar scowled.

"Scouts," said Isabel. "Sent to gather information."

"On the enemy scout," said Tork.

Isabel nodded. "A second team disappeared, as well. An hour ago, the station went silent, too. Our assessment at this time..." Her frown deepened. "...is that Io may have been lost."

"Now I understand." Angar swung his feet up on the table and wrapped his arms around his knees. "This is a *suicide mission.*"

Isabel shook her head. "No, that's..."

"You're going out in a blaze of glory against the enemy you can't defeat." Angar grinned. "One last act of courage before you die and awaken in the Never-Ending War."

Isabel whirled to face him and raised her voice. "*Wrong.* This is just the *beginning.*" Marching over, she shoved his legs hard, knocking him off balance. "Now get your damn *feet* off the *table!*" She shoved him again.

Angar grimaced but did as she told him.

"We are going to Io to take it back," said Isabel. "And hand the Caul their first *defeat.* But it won't be the *last.*" She leaned in close, barking her words at Angar and Tork. "It will be the start of our campaign to *expunge* them from the *galaxy.*"

"You're a *dreamer.*" Angar laughed. "What makes you think *you* can beat the Caul when so many others have *failed?*"

"This ship." She said it with absolute conviction. "Its crew. The Undoing. And the two of you."

Angar looked at Tork and laughed. "The *two* of us? Is that a *joke?*"

Suddenly, Isabel lunged forward and slapped him across the face. "Shut your mouth!" she shouted.

Angar reached up to touch his face and gaped at her in utter disbelief. Tork did the same. He'd never in his life seen a woman strike Angar like that, not even one of his wives.

If Isabel felt the slightest bit afraid, she didn't show it. If anything, she leaned in closer to Angar.

"You two, *both* of you, have a chance to save *everything,*" she said sharply. "You can have a destiny *far greater* than hacking each other to *pieces* on a primitive *mudball* until the Caul comes to tear you to *shreds*. Or you can keep acting like petulant *children* and let it all go to *hell*. *Your choice*. But *I* won't stop *fighting* until I draw my last *breath*."

With that, she spun and hit buttons on the control board. The hovering image zoomed out and swooped over to show the icon for the *Hellcyon* between Jupiter and Mars.

"Now let's get back to business," she said stiffly. "I'm going to put you through a mind's-eye simulation like we did before, when you seemed to fly down to Earth and back up to the ship. Consider yourselves warned."

"No, wait..." said Angar.

But it was too late. "Pay attention to the details and try not to get sick." Isabel punched a red button on the board.

And Tork couldn't help crying out as the room around him seemed to disappear, leaving him and Angar floating in space.

JUST LIKE THE FIRST SIMULATION, everything looked and felt utterly real to Tork. Drifting in space, he felt weightless and cold, without the slightest control over his motion—a feeling he hated. He was used to ruling his own body and determining how it moved next, not having some outside force maneuver him as it chose.

But, suddenly, he didn't mind the direction he was moving. As he turned and rolled, an object came into view above him, shockingly massive and powerful-looking.

It glided over him, its gargantuan, dark metal bulk blotting out the stars. At the front, an enormous death's-head skull glowed fiercely red, its giant horns curling down and back up to gleaming black points like the rack on a bighorn sheep.

A long, sleek body came next, molded from the same dark metal. Three back-swept spines jutted from the torso on either side, all pointing up and back at the rear assembly that followed.

At the base of the torso, a square, open bay glowed with crimson light, a cavity in the front of the rearward section. The rear section itself was astonishingly wide—a vast span of two fixed wings with a monstrous block of engines in the middle. As the thing passed, Tork could see all four of those engines blaze with fiery red-orange light, brighter than the sun on a blistering hot late summer day in the desert back home.

It was only then, as it passed, and the guiding force of the simulation lifted him up and after it, that he realized what he was looking at. That massive, fearsome thing was a *ship*; it must be the very ship he was riding in.

For the first time, Tork was seeing what the *Hellcyon* looked like from outside.

His heart pounded, then, as he swooped up and over the vessel, rising so he was now looking down at it. Angar joined him, soaring up alongside him, and they shared a wide-eyed, exhilarated look. For once, neither of them was angry or suspicious or scheming; they were caught up in the wonder of that enormous vessel racing below them, its fierce red skull and spines making it look spectacular as well as ferocious.

Then, they accelerated and leaped away from it,

propelled at incredible speeds toward Jupiter and its pale moon, Io.

Tork held his breath as Io swiftly enlarged before him, zooming up so fast he thought he might collide with it. Then, he and Angar slowed dramatically, gliding down to the yellow and rust surface with its scattered dark pockmarks.

As they got closer, Tork saw that some of the pockmarks were volcanoes, spewing fiery streams into the sky. One came to life just as he passed over it, belching up a cloud of ash and flame that only missed him by fractions of a second.

Soaring low over the curve of the moon, Tork saw an artificial structure in the distance, a gleaming, transparent dome sprawling on a dusty yellow plain. As he approached it, he saw a cluster of squat buildings inside, fashioned from yellow stone and set with glinting glass windows and solar panels.

Tork and Angar banked and swept away from the dome, cruising toward a range of hills with Jupiter's red spot swelling behind them. Several hilltops flicked away, and then they saw it—a glowing object on the rust-colored ground, pulsing as they watched...and changing shape with each pulse. It looked like a mass of silver liquid, crackling with arcs of lightning. It pulsed as if driven by a heart, and with each pulse, it took on a new shape—a thorny sphere, a cube, a snowflake, a mobius strip, an inverted pyramid, a star. At one point, it became an oblong shape with a tapered tip, and Tork thought it must be the enemy scout ship—though he couldn't be sure.

Then, as he and Angar slid closer, something exploded from inside the silver mass, bursting into the sky and flashing past them in a wild, flickering blur. It churned toward the dome so fast, it made Tork and Angar look like they were standing still, hovering in one place.

Mesmerized, Tork and Angar watched as the blur crashed into the dome with shuddering force, blowing a hole in the gleaming, smooth surface. Seconds later, buildings inside the domed structure erupted in a series of blasts, a chain reaction of fiery destruction.

Tork gazed into the flames as each new explosion pounded the station. One thought flashed through his brain in those moments, just before he and Angar were wrenched from the site and shot back through space to the waiting *Hellcyon* in their shared simulation.

How in the name of Yorg can we possibly beat that?

19

ANGAR STOOD in the prow of the *Hellcyon*—what the crew called the Skull—gazing out through one of the eyes in the fiery death's head. He had the run of the ship now, more or less, though whatever science tricks the Blacksmiths had planted inside him still kept him from entering certain places. *No matter,* he thought. *I'll find a way to conquer* everything *sooner or later.*

The stars flashed by quickly, seeming to part before him like waves before the prow of a boat on the water. *Hellcyon* was flying as fast as it could to the next rip point; for reasons he didn't understand, the ship had to open and enter rips at certain locations to make it to the destination without going off-course.

Angar shook his head at the strangeness of it all, which he couldn't grasp. As much as the Blacksmiths called it science, it might as well have been magic to him. That was how he processed what they told him, framing it in the context of magic spells and forces.

Whatever the power behind it, he would make it his own soon enough. That was what he'd done all his life, seizing what others had—except Tork. But even *that* lump of shit would grovel before him soon enough; even Tork would surrender his power and pledge lifelong servitude when this was all over.

Was it possible to have *too much* power? Thanks to the Blacksmiths, he would soon find out. Plans were already forming in his mind to make his supreme dominance a reality.

Angar smiled at the thought of it.

Just then, he heard footsteps behind him and whirled with fists clenched to dispatch whatever enemy was sneaking up on him.

The glowing girl who stood there did not seem the slightest bit afraid of him.

"Hello." She was diminutive, two heads smaller than Angar. Her face was round, her features elfin, her skin glowing with pale white light and flowing with swirls of color. Slender, fuzzy antennae tipped with tiny gold beads rose at her temples, swaying from the fall of multicolored petals that draped her head and shoulders.

"Hello." Angar froze, mesmerized by her unearthly beauty. For once, he didn't know what to say.

"I am Lieutenant Quinza Acquiesce." Her voice had a chiming sound, melodic and soothing. As she smiled, the petals on her head came to life, fluttering and rising in the air.

It was then that Angar realized they weren't petals at all but the brightly-colored wings of butterflies. As he stood there, dumbfounded, they fluttered over and wheeled around him, their wings caressing him with tiny breezes.

His mouth fell open. He had never seen anything like it before. He had never seen any*one* like *her* before.

"And which one are you?" Quinza looked amused. "The one who defeated an entire training class single-handedly?"

He nodded. "I am Angar Crux." That was all he managed to get out.

"Yes, you are, aren't you?" Quinza giggled. "And I, for one, am *very* glad you're on *our* side." She cocked her head to one side and narrowed her bright yellow eyes. "Or *are* you?"

Angar shrugged. "I don't seem to have a choice in the matter."

"Is that so?" She waved her hands, and several of the butterflies landed on Angar's head and shoulders, then sat there, wings softly rising and falling. "You have no preference, then? No other intentions in mind?"

As she spoke, Angar felt a tingling where the butterflies sat, and he began to wonder about their purpose. Were they doing something to him? Were they somehow extensions of *her?*

Suddenly agitated, he shook his head hard and shooed them away. The butterflies flew around him for another moment, then returned to their roost on Quinza's head with all the others.

"Too bad you're so restless," she said. "I think they like you."

"I'm not a *perch* for *bugs*," snapped Angar. "And I won't have my *loyalties* questioned."

"As you wish." Smiling to herself and humming softly, Quinza stepped over to stand beside him, gazing out the window in the death's head's eye. "That wasn't why I came here tonight, anyway. I'm off-duty, to be honest."

"Off duty?"

Quinza nodded. "And this is my happy place."

Angar frowned. "Happy place?"

Her laugh was like the chiming of a little bell. "*You* know. A place I go to feel good and forget my troubles. A place where I can be myself."

"This place makes you feel good?" asked Angar.

The light of the window glowed on her skin, casting all the swirls of color in shades of red. "How could it not, with so much *beauty* out there? And so much *peace* and *quiet* in here?"

Beauty, peace, and quiet weren't things that Angar treasured, but he nodded as if in agreement. Something about Quinza made him feel at ease, in spite of the raging ambition that churned away in his heart.

"What's *your* happy place?" she asked. "Where do *you* feel good?"

He thought for a moment, then grunted. "On the battlefield," he said. "In the middle of a battle against a worthy enemy."

Quinza smiled at him but didn't laugh. "I wonder if there are other places where you might also feel good, Angar? Places where blood isn't being spilled?"

Looking at her, he felt that tingle again, but none of the butterflies were anywhere near him. Was she a witch, he wondered, casting some kind of magic spell to soften his heart?

Or was the truth of his attraction much simpler than that?

"No," he said. "I can't think of a place like that."

"Not even at home with your wives?" Quinza returned her gaze to the starfield. "You have five of them, don't you?"

"Seven." The question rankled him. Had she come to the Skull because it was her happy place, or because she wanted to interrogate him?

"I'll bet you miss them very much." Her butterflies fluttered their wings as she said it.

Not really, he thought, but he didn't say it. What was happening out there among the stars was so much more important than his family life, it did not compare.

"I have no one to miss," Quinza said softly, reaching out to touch the window. "I am the last of my kind."

He felt a sudden burst of an unfamiliar emotion—what he might have thought of as *compassion* if he'd known what that was. "How did you escape?"

"My people sacrificed much," said Quinza. "I was so important to them, they paid the ultimate price to get me to the waiting arms of The Undoing."

"Important?" asked Angar. "Why? Who were you to them?"

"What if I told you I was a goddess?" Her eyes sparkled, and her butterflies fluttered.

"Are you?"

She shrugged. "It doesn't matter anymore. Everyone and everything I have left is on this ship. It is my whole world now, and no one worships me here."

With that, she turned and walked away from him,

heading for the door into the corridor. The way she glided over the floor, her every movement smooth and graceful, he found he couldn't look away.

"Will I see you again?" he asked. "Here, in your...happy place?"

Quinza looked over her shoulder at him, antennae bobbing. "That is up to you." She grinned. "Now I really must excuse myself and return to duty."

"Duty." Angar felt like he'd say or do almost anything to keep her there. "What did you say your duty is, exactly?"

Quinza laughed. "It's a surprise," she said, and then she glided to the door, and it opened to let her out.

Leaving Angar alone in the Skull, gazing after her with a stupefied expression as if he'd been struck in the head with a heavy object.

20

TORK COULDN'T STOP the smile of pure pleasure from curling across his face.

He had never before held a battle axe of such exquisite design, the curved blade like that of a crescent moon, the heel extruded in a perfect spike like the fang of a great beast. A round, crimson gem was set between them like a baleful eye, emitting crackling streams of energy that crawled along the metal. As for the handle, it was perfectly balanced, curved along the length and hooked slightly at the base to strengthen the grip.

The axe was so well-fashioned, in fact, that it sang as he swung it before him. It left a trail of energy streams, too, that snaked and flickered in midair. The whole weapon felt instantly at one with him, magnificently attuned to his every physical feature and the depths of his warrior's nature.

"What do you think?" asked Gauge, who was watching expectantly. "Does it suit you?"

Tork swung it through the air again, delighting in the steady stroke that would easily slice through flesh and bone alike. "It's all right, I suppose."

"Remember, it's linked to your genome." The armorer, Lieutenant Zeezo Skeezik—a reptilian/fungal creature with moldy/scaly skin—pointed one long, black claw at the axe. "Only *you* can use it without being fatally *electrocuted.*"

"I'll try to keep that in mind." As bored as Tork sounded, he doubted Gauge and Skeezik would ever guess how excited he really was. The axe was a dream, so far beyond his old weapons that he couldn't imagine ever wielding them again. "If this is the best you can do, I'll just have to make the best of it."

"That's true," said Gauge. "It will have to do, since we're arriving at Io in less than a day."

Just then, the door swept open, and Angar stomped into the armory, scowling. On his way across the big room, he knocked over a set of pikes, sending them clattering to the floor behind him without turning to pick them up.

"I was told to come here," he said stiffly. "What do you people want?"

"We're arming you," said Gauge. "Giving you weapons for your mission. You'll want to practice with them before we get in range of Io."

Angar sneered. "Practice?"

"Get the feel of them." Skeezik grabbed a broadsword from his workbench and offered it to him. "It can only give you an edge against the enemy."

Angar eyed the long blade as it gleamed in the overhead lighting. "This wasn't forged by the metal masters of the Eastern Horde, was it?"

"*I* forged it," said Skeezik, flickering his forked, pasty tongue.

Angar snorted. "Obviously."

When Skeezik pressed the grip at him, however, Angar wrapped his thick-fingered hand around it. Frowning, he flipped the sword from side to side, testing the heft, watching the play of light over the blade.

"Inferior." When he said it, he slashed the sword through the air in a fast figure eight, then stabbed it at Tork's abdomen.

Tork swung up the axe and blocked the strike, holding fast just inches from his belly. "Maybe the problem is with the *man*, not the *weapon*."

Laughing, Angar wrenched the sword free and swept it around, aiming at Tork's throat. The blade flashed in at unbelievable speed, but Tork still whipped up the axe and deflected it. Metal clanged loudly as the two weapons clashed, colliding with such force that they shivered between the barbarians.

"Angar, stop!" said Gauge. "Tork! Enough!"

His calls did not get through to them. They broke the clinch again, stood motionless for a moment...and *exploded* in a flurry of ringing blows, one after another.

Sword and axe crashed together again and again, blades battering each other remorselessly. It was as if the two men were fighting to the death back home on Earth, pounding each other in one final winner-take-all match for dominance of all the hordes.

"Yield!" shouted Tork through clenched teeth, heaving aside another blow from the broadsword.

Angar's grin and a fresh volley of strikes were his only answer. The last of those were so fierce, they staggered Tork, pressing him back three steps.

After which, the sword swung back and lashed forward with the greatest strike yet, one that seemed as if it nearly broke through.

"Stop!" said Gauge. "You'll only hurt yourselves!"

If that was a worry to Angar, he didn't show it. If anything, he redoubled his efforts, hacking with the sword from every angle.

It was then that Tork knew without a doubt that Angar's hatred hadn't waned. Tork had gotten caught up in the world of the ship and the mission to save the galaxy...but Angar's desire to kill him was unabated. Fury blazed in his eyes with all the heat of the volcanoes of Io, beyond all sense and any measure of self-preservation.

Again, the sword came down, and again. The power behind those blows stunned Tork and wore him down, though he knew he couldn't show weakness for even an instant.

Would he do it if he could? Would Angar kill him, though it meant killing himself too because of the Blacksmiths' blowback science?

Tork didn't get to find out, because the two of them suddenly froze in mid-battle. Tork's axe was upraised, Angar's sword was thrusting at his heart, and both were locked in place like statues in the middle of the armory.

"I said that's enough." Gauge stepped forward, looking deeply unhappy, and tweaked buttons on a silver control board. Slowly, the barbarians lowered their weapons, moving against their will, until the blades touched the floor. They straightened, standing at attention as Gauge passed between them.

"Yorg...*curse* you...Blacksmith," hissed Angar, so stressed at the loss of control that he looked like he might blow a blood vessel.

"Quiet." Gauge played the buttons again, and Angar fell silent. "Now listen to me."

Angar clamped his eyes shut, grunting and straining against the controller.

Gauge flipped a switch. *"I said listen!"* Suddenly, his voice boomed in Tork's head. Angar winced, looking as if the voice was blasting in his skull, too.

"That's right! I'm communicating directly with your brains!" Gauge didn't make a sound or move his lips, but his voice came through loud and clear in Tork's head. "It's called the *thinklink*, and you can't shut it off. It's how we'll communicate with you during the mission."

Angar winced harder, then relaxed. His eyes fell shut, and he smiled.

Suddenly, his own voice erupted in Angar's head across the thinklink. *"GET OUT OF MY HEAD OR I'LL KILL YOU!"*

He started to say something else and was cut off.

"Quiet, I said!" Gauge's voice was the only one talking now. *"And listen to what I tell you! Save the savagery for the enemy! You'll have plenty of chances to let off steam on Io."*

Angar twitched, fighting again, but the Blacksmith's power wouldn't release him or let him speak.

"You want to kill each other so badly?" said Gauge. *"If you*

do, you'll be killing all your people, too! Make no mistake, the Caul are coming for them! The Southern and Eastern hordes alike, and all others besides.

"Do you understand? If you don't stop the Caul, everyone you care about, everyone you rule, will die at their hands. All of them!"

With that, suddenly, Tork felt his body unlock. Angar began moving freely, too.

"Your people *need* you." This time, Gauge's voice was in their ears, not their minds. "So get your *shit* together or live the rest of your lives knowing they all *died* because of *you.*"

Tork and Angar were no longer held silent by Blacksmith science, but neither said a word. Gauge glaring at them both with contempt, then took a deep breath and slowly released it, looking calmer.

"Think about what I said," he told them. "And remember you have that training session in the gym in an hour. Angar, I want *you* serving as lead instructor."

"Me?" said Angar.

"No arguments!" snapped Gauge. "Or you'll learn about the *kill switch* implanted in your skulls the *hard* way!" With that, he marched out of the armory, leaving them alone with the armorer.

"So, gentlemen." Skeezik cleared his throat and winked one silvery reptilian eye. "Would you like me to try your hand at some other weapons I've got in stock?"

"What other weapons?" Angar sounded sulky.

"Have you ever fired a *gun* before?" Skeezik opened a long black case on his workbench.

"I don't know," said Tork. "What's a—"

"*This.*" Skeezik lifted an object from the case, a black metal tool the length of his arm. One end was a skinny metal cylinder, the other a triangular butt with a padded base. "It's what we call a rifle. A *burner* rifle, to be exact."

Raising the rifle, he fit the butt against his shoulder, gazed along the length of the cylindrical nose, and squeezed the crescent-shaped switch mounted along the bottom of the object.

Instantly, a jet of searing yellow energy poured from the nose, slicing a charred gash in the bulkhead across the room.

"And *that's* what it can do on its lowest setting!" Skeezik released the trigger, and the energy stream ceased instantly. "So who wants to try a little target practice down at the range?"

"Me!" Angar seemed noticeably cheerier. "I do!"

Skeezik gave him the rifle. Tork raised his hand to volunteer, too, though he wasn't quite as enthusiastic as Angar was.

"Awesome!" Skeezik pulled another rifle from the case and tossed it to him. "Just don't turn them on *each other,* okay?"

"Okay," said Tork, handling the rifle carefully.

"Wouldn't dream of it," said Angar as he pointed his rifle at Tork and sighted along the length of it at his head. "The thought never entered my mind for even a *second.*"

Then, though he'd never used a rifle before, he pretended to shoot it like Skeezik had done, right between Tork's eyes.

"Target practice." Angar grinned and chuckled. "Yes, I think I'd like that."

"Excellent," said Skeezik. "And wait till you see what happens when you power up the sword and axe."

"Power up?" asked Tork.

"Sure." Skeezik chuckled. "You didn't think I'd give you a non-electrified weapon, did you?"

BEFORE

EARTH, 10 YEARS AGO

As the music of the drums and stringed instruments played, Tork and Angar took turns dancing with Lillia under the starry night sky, grinning as they inhaled her sweet scent. Other members of the Grand and Glorious Horde danced and laughed and clapped, too, wheeling and stomping around the roaring fire in the heart of their camp.

"I love your people!" Lillia beamed as Tork spun her around. "They're so full of joy! And they've been so welcoming! I can't believe your Horde Lord had this festival in my honor!"

"Scalder Pacious is a great lord, all right," said Angar as he cut in, sweeping her around in a kind of rough waltz. "Greatest of them all! And he has raised Tork and me as his own from the time we were babes."

"The Raiders who kidnapped me are nothing like that." Lillia's face darkened. "They are the foulest of the foul, dedicated to the most unspeakable of deeds."

"How long were you their captive?" asked Angar.

"*Years.*" *Lillia scowled, then brightened.* "*But that doesn't matter anymore. Thanks to the two of you, I'm finally free.*"

Just then, Tork tried to cut in, taking her hand and trying to pull her away, but Angar wouldn't let go. The three of them jostled awkwardly for a moment...and then the music stopped, and the other dancers applauded.

It took a moment more, however, for Tork and Angar to let go of Lillia and stop glaring at each other.

"*Everyone!*" *With the flames leaping behind him, Scalder Pacious raised his muscular arms in the air. His bushy hair and beard were flecked with gray, but he was still a formidable figure, a towering warrior with bulging muscles who instantly commanded attention and respect.* "*This young woman has asked for asylum among us! I will do her one better and invite her to join our horde on a permanent basis! Are you with me?*"

Everyone around the fire roared in agreement—none louder than Tork and Angar.

"*I have my answer!*" *shouted Scalder.* "*And what say you, fair Lillia?*"

Tears rolled from Lillia's eyes, and she swiped them away. "*I can't thank you enough, Lord Pacious.*" *She looked overcome with joy and sadness all at once.* "*I accept. Of course, I accept!*"

With that, everyone cheered with approval, and the music started playing again.

"*This is wonderful, Lillia,*" *said Tork.* "*May I have this dance to celebrate?*"

"*May I have this dance?*" *asked Angar.*

"*Thank you both, but I'm exhausted. I really need some sleep.*" *Smiling, she hopped up to kiss Tork on the cheek, then did the same for Angar.* "*Good night to you both, my good, strong men.*"

Then, with a last wave for them both, she headed off to the tent they'd set up for her after saving her from the Raiders that morning.

As soon as she disappeared inside, Angar turned and glared at Tork. "She likes me best," he said coldly. "You need to back off."

Tork frowned. "I didn't hear her say that. If anything, I'd say she likes me best."

Angar's hand lashed out and clamped down on Tork's shoulder, not in a friendly way. "Very funny. Didn't you see how she was looking *at me?"*

"Didn't you *see how she was looking at* me?*"*

Angar squeezed Tork's shoulder so hard, it hurt. "You can't have her. She's mine."

Tork broke free of his grip. "She will never *be yours."*

And with that, the two crashed together, fighting over a woman for the first time in their lives. Grunting, punching, and wrestling, they struggled against each other, vying for dominance though they were evenly matched in every way.

Then, finally, Scalder Pacious stormed over and broke up the fight. "Enough! What are you fighting over?"

"Her." A young woman stepped out of the crowd, clad in a crimson cloak, her long black hair streaming in the wind. She was Vixa, daughter of the witch Igli. "They are fighting over the girl, Lillia."

Scalder laughed. "Is that *all?" He smacked Tork and Angar both on the back. "It figures, these hot-blooded young men."*

"She has then mesmerized with her power." Vixa raised an index finger. "Make light of it at your peril," she said grimly. "For that woman is a bitch-goddess, and she will be your undoing."

Young and unproven as Vixa was, no one took her seriously. They laughed, and she marched off into the night without another word.

But Tork and Angar weren't laughing at all. Though Scalder stood between them, keeping them apart, they stood there stiffly and glared, their newfound animosity unresolved.

21

When Angar entered the gym, he could feel the tension rise among the crowd of people waiting there. All eyes instantly turned to him, and every muscle tightened. They all knew what he'd done during the first training session, even those who hadn't been there, and they feared what he might do next.

Mostly, he was glad for the fear and respect. It would make things so much easier when the time came to seize power.

But for what he had to do next, at Io, he had to temper that fear. Raging unpredictability might be amusing and helpful in a mutiny, but it might not serve him so well on a dangerous mission requiring team effort.

And the truth was, Gauge was right about the importance of the mission. Angar knew he had to defeat the enemy on that moon, or risk losing his horde back home.

As much as it galled him, he was part of the Blacksmiths' war.

Standing in front of the crowd of fifty-plus students, he cleared his throat loudly...not that he had to. No one else was saying a word; he had their undivided attention for as long as he wanted it.

"I've been told to come here," he said, as roughly as ever. "To apologize and train you the *right* way, whatever that is. Well, you can *forget* the apology.

"I did what I did to make you *hate*. So did it work?"

For a moment, no one in the gym said a word. Some people shuffled their feet, others looked away, a few muttered, but no one spoke.

"Come on now!" Angar laughed. "None of you hate me, after what I did to you? *None* of you?"

Again, no one spoke. It was then that the door slid open, admitting Tork and Gauge.

Angar ignored them. "So it's *true*, then. You people really *have* lost your killer instinct. You won't strike back when someone *hurts* you."

Someone in the back of the room coughed. Otherwise, no one made a sound.

"Then you're all *hopeless*," said Angar. "And *doomed*. If you won't stand up to *one man*, how can you ever stand up to the *Caul?*"

Suddenly, a man at the front of the group stepped forward. He looked like he was cut from ruby crystal, swirling inside with sparks and mist.

"You're wrong," he said, his voice firm and strong. "Someone *will* stand up to you."

Angar chuckled. "Good for you. At least *one* of you isn't a *coward*."

The ruby crystal man shook his head. "*Not* one." As he

said it, he flung back an arm and gestured behind him. "*All.*"

Without a word, the whole crowd rushed forward at once, heading straight for Angar. Completely taken by surprise, he batted away the first few, but the others kept coming. They overwhelmed him with sheer numbers, knocking him back to the floor and pinning him there with the combined weight of their bodies.

Blows rained down upon Angar, and he deflected them —but didn't fight back. On a battlefield, he would have surged up and heaved them all away without much effort...but he was all too conscious of the presence of Gauge in the room, judging him. He didn't want to get any further on Gauge's bad side after the fight in the armory. Not to mention, the cryptic mention of a "kill switch" in his head had him worried.

So Angar held back and let the students have their fun. He let himself be their punching bag just long enough to make it look good.

Then, as they began to withdraw, he got up from the floor and glared at them. They shrank from his gaze, but just a little.

"Whose idea was that?" he asked angrily. "*Whose?*"

Everyone raised a hand (or comparable appendage) at once.

Angar stormed over to confront the ruby crystal man. "It was *your* idea, though, wasn't it? You're their *leader*."

The ruby man met his gaze. "Does it matter?"

Gauge interrupted by clearing his throat. "Of course it does, Major Schist. It makes you the perfect candidate."

"For what?" asked Schist.

"Leading his team." Gauge gestured at Angar. "You'll be his second in command."

Schist's crystal turned from ruby red to fiery orange. "But I...that's not...I don't..."

"You have your orders," barked Gauge, and then he whirled on Angar. "*Both* of you."

Angar seethed. "I don't *need*..."

"You need what I *say* you need," snapped Gauge. "Now teach your class."

The usual rage boiled up within Angar, pressing at the thin walls of his self-control. He desperately wanted to lash out and show *everyone* his dominance and power, no matter the cost.

But then he looked back at Tork, who was leaning against the wall, watching...and smirking. Tork, he realized, was getting ahead by playing along...positioning himself, no doubt, for his own big move.

Was Angar going to let him get away with that?

"All right." Angar marched over to Schist and clapped him on his hard, crystalline shoulder. "I say welcome aboard, sub-lord! Together, we will *slaughter* the foul Caul!"

Schist changed color back to red, then yellow, and he nodded without smiling, still looking uneasy.

Angar, for his part, took the man's measure as he squeezed his shoulder, deciding how best to shatter him when the time came.

He did the same for every member of his team when Gauge had finished selecting them...and the same again for every member of Tork's team when they had also been chosen.

All the while, he kept a phony mask of cooperation firmly in place, revealing nothing of his true intentions to anyone present.

Or so he hoped.

22

ISABEL PUSHED the big glass helmet at Tork for the third time. "If you *want* to die in space, be my guest," she said. "Otherwise, you need to put this on!"

Tork shook his head. He already wore the rest of the space suit, and it made him acutely uncomfortable; putting on the helmet was a bridge too far.

He thought she ought to be grateful, actually. Angar hadn't even put on the suit yet. As cooperative as he'd been in the gym an hour ago, he flat-out refused to obey Isabel's instructions to suit up in the *Hellcyon*'s launch bay.

"I can't *fight* with that thing on my head," said Tork. "I can't fight with *any* of this on!" He smacked his palms against the chest of his armored black suit, which clanked when he struck it. "You want to sentence us to *death* on the battlefield?"

"You won't even *get* to the fight if you don't wear *this*." Isabel pushed the helmet at him again. "As I *explained* to you *both*, you can't *breathe* in space without an environment suit and helmet with a built-in air supply. It's that *simple*."

Tork scowled. He looked around the busy bay for support, but none of the dozens of men, women, and creatures scurrying about their business paid any attention. "But if you drop us off right on Io..."

"For the third time...*no*." Isabel blew out her breath in frustration, making her feathery black bangs flutter. "It's the *same* on Io. No *air*, except in the dome, and the dome's been compromised."

"Then what about some kind of...mask?" asked Tork. "Something we can breathe from without the helmet and all *this* getting in the way?"

"Because," said Isabel. "As I've already *explained* to you, it's *not just* the air that's the *problem*. The lack of *pressure* could make your bodies *explode*. Then there's the cosmic radiation that could cook you alive. You need the whole suit, helmet and all."

Though Tork understood what she was saying, he wanted nothing to do with the space suit. He waved her off and turned, intending to leave the launch bay—only to come face to face with Angar.

"I just realized, she's right," said Angar. "We need to listen to what she says."

Tork scowled. "Since when are *you* the voice of reason?"

"Since *she* told us how *space* works." Angar hiked a thumb in Isabel's direction. "This might be a suicide mission, but I'm not going to *kill* myself for a *stupid* reason."

Tork's blood boiled, then subsided. Giving Angar any

kind of edge was something he didn't want to do. "You're right, Horde Lord."

Turning, he walked over and accepted the helmet from Isabel. She watched as he tried to put it on, then sighed and helped him get it screwed into place.

When she clapped the glowing green dial on the chest of his suit and tinkered with knobs on the air supply backpack, fresh air rushed into the helmet.

"There you go." Isabel walked around him, checking various seals, and nodded. "Now let's get your partner squared away."

Moments later, both men stood in the middle of the launch bay in their black suits and helmets, glaring at each other.

"Good, good." She pressed a button on her control board, and a siren blared through the launch bay. The many crew members at work in the vast chamber stopped what they were doing and hurried for the doors.

"What's going on?" Angar's voice was muffled by the helmet.

"Just clearing the room." Isabel walked over to the wall and grabbed two poles she'd left leaning there, each tipped on both ends with padded blue disks. "It's time for a little zero-G sparring. Winner gets an attaboy."

"Attaboy?" Angar frowned.

Isabel tossed the paddles to each of them in turn, then headed for the door.

"Zero *what?*" asked Tork.

"You'll see," Isabel said over her shoulder, and then the door swept shut behind her.

"Sparring, huh?" Angar spun his paddle in his hand,

then flipped it aloft and caught it. He lunged forward, jabbing the paddle at Tork's midsection. "Sounds amusing...for a *little* while, anyway."

No sooner had he said it than his feet left the ground. Off-balance, he pinwheeled his arms, dropping the paddle.

Which then proceeded to drift off toward the ceiling.

"What *is* this?" yelled Angar. "What's happening?"

Tork adjusted faster as he, too, floated upward. Instead of scrambling, he let himself drift and roll. The paddle never left his hands.

"This must be zero-G." Looking around, Tork saw objects floating, too, rising from the deck plates like birds taking wing. He would have to be careful, he realized, or risk colliding with one of them.

Suddenly, Isabel's voice piped up in his head via thinklink. "This is as close as you'll get aboard ship to conditions *outside* the ship—zero gravity, no atmosphere, low pressure. If you compromise your environment suits, you'll die."

"She wouldn't dare let that happen," said Angar over the thinklink.

"Yes, I would," snapped Isabel. "Now get sparring. You need the practice."

"We don't need *any-*" said Angar.

Isabel cut him off. "Fighting under these conditions is *very* different from what you're used to. You *need* the practice. Not to mention, it's fun."

Just as those words flowed through the link, Tork pushed off from a floating cargo container and leaped toward Angar. Before Angar even saw him coming, he smacked him in the hindquarters with the paddle. Thanks to their blowback connection, he felt the blow as much as Angar, but it was worth it.

Angar cried out with irritation and clumsily turned for a swing at his opponent...but it was too late. The force of the swat had thrown Tork in another direction, scudding across the bay.

"Not so easy, is it?" said Isabel. "You have to use your acrobatic skills and see the battlefield as a sphere instead of a plain."

Tork was a natural, kicking off from a bulkhead and somersaulting toward another drifting cargo box. He caught it with both feet and propelled it straight toward Angar.

Angar saw it coming but didn't have anything to throw at it. He settled for ducking at the last second, flipping himself over in time to avoid a collision.

As the container tumbled past, Angar spotted a fork-lift drifting nearby, coming toward him. It came just close enough for him to grab one tine of the fork and use it to swing himself around and flick off toward a bulkhead.

He wasn't as adept as Tork, but he managed to twist around and get in a good kick off the bulkhead. Sailing across the bay, he snagged his paddle from where it floated and used it to push off a passing cabinet, redirecting his flight.

With that, Angar made a beeline for Tork, who was floating near the ceiling—but Tork saw him and swung around his own paddle, deflecting the shot. Knocked away, Angar tumbled aside, where he struck a floating computer bank and bounced away toward a cluster of objects—more equipment and containers circling a spherical carrier like planets orbiting the sun.

Angar couldn't stop himself from crashing through the cluster of objects. They battered him from all sides, leaving him stunned—setting him up for another attack.

The echo of the pain left Tork dazed for an instant, but he quickly recovered and launched himself back into play.

When Tork flashed toward him, Angar batted the spherical carrier with his paddle, putting everything he had into the shot. The carrier hurtled at Tork, thudding into his chest so hard, it threw him backward. He bounced off a piece of equipment, then spun into a bulkhead, losing his paddle on the way.

At which point, even with the blowback pain flaring, Angar roared with laughter, happy to finally have the upper hand.

"I think I'm getting the hang of this!" he said across the thinklink. "And you're right, Isabel. This zero-G fighting *is* fun!"

"Good to hear," said Isabel. "But remember, this is just a simulation of what it's *really* like."

"I can't wait to try the *real* version, then." Angar kept laughing through the link. "So I can see Tork fail even more!"

"Laugh while you can," said Tork. "You're about to take some serious hits."

"Bring it on!" Angar kicked off another bulkhead with his paddle raised high, not even thinking about the fact that he was fighting in a bulky helmet and space suit.

BEFORE

EARTH, 10 YEARS AGO

The MORNING *after the festival in honor of Lillia joining the Grand and Glorious Horde, Tork went to see her. Angar was already there, peering into her tent.*

"She's not here." Angar let the flap fall shut and shrugged. "Maybe she went for a walk."

Tork scanned the ground, squinting at the dry gray dust. "There." He pointed. "I see tracks."

Angar took a look as well. "They're hers, all right. Heading off into the hills."

The two of them set out, tracking her together though each of them wanted her to himself.

The tracks led them along a winding trail between the low hills that lay behind camp. At first, they showed she'd been running—but after a while, it was clear she'd slowed down to a walking pace.

Further on, she left the trail, striking out into the open waste. It was there they finally spotted her, walking fast under gathering dark clouds.

They ran to catch up, shouting her name, and she turned...but she didn't look happy to see them.

"Hey, Lillia!" Angar trotted over with a wave. He couldn't help smiling when he caught a whiff of her sweet fragrance. "Where are you going?"

"Getting some exercise?" asked Tork as he ran up beside her, also breathing deep of her perfume.

Before Lillia could say a word, a distant scream pierced the air...then another, and another.

Angar stared in the direction of the screams, the direction from which they'd come. "What the shang?"

"They're coming from camp." Tork frowned. "Something's happened."

The next scream that tore through the air was a recognizable word, a single syllable that set both men's hair on edge: KEEEEE.

It could only mean one thing. "Someone's dead!" said Angar. "But who?"

Tork met his gaze, and a world of meaning passed between them. They both knew the screams were for someone important. Death was such an everyday occurrence in their harsh world, it would never lead to screams like that for someone ordinary.

Another scream rose in the distance, and another.

It was then that Lillia finally spoke. "You already know who's dead. After all, it was you who killed him."

Angar scowled at her, utterly confused. "What are you talking about?"

"Your horde lord, Scalder Pacious," said Lillia. "He came to me last night. He tried to have me. And you stopped him—but you went too far. You killed him."

"Wait—him?" Angar pointed at Tork.

Tork jabbed a finger at Angar. "You mean him?"

"But I didn't!" snapped Angar.

"I would never!" said Tork.

"Liar!" Lillia shook her head with disgust. "You know you did it. I know you did it."

"Did you?" Angar's disbelief was turning to rage as he lunged in front of Tork.

"Don't try to blame me!" said Tork.

"You both wanted me," said Lillia. "Now neither of you can have me. And you're about to lose everything else you've ever loved besides, with your great leader dead."

Suddenly, they heard something new in the distance: the thunder of hoofbeats.

Looking across the wastes, they glimpsed a huge group of horses, all with riders, charging toward camp. Weapons gleaming, torches blazing, they hurtled toward the Grand and Glorious Horde at breakneck speed.

"You'd better get going," said Lillia. "Work out your differences later."

"Wait." Tork pushed past Angar and stormed toward her. "You did it, didn't you? Neither of us would ever harm our Horde Lord."

"That's exactly what we'd expect you to say, isn't it?" Lillie dug a handful of golden glitter from a pocket of frock and blew it at them.

Angar's eyes rolled up in their sockets as he breathed in the glitter. "It is!" he said, turning toward Tork.

Dazed, Tork tried waving away the glitter and shook his head hard. "What would you...expect me to say...?"

Laughing, Lillia strutted over to them. Her heavy, sweet scent clouded the air around them as she leaned in to whisper in

Angar's ear. "He did it," she said, pointing at Tork. "Never forget, never forgive."

Then, giggling with delight, she said the same things into Tork's ear, pointing at Angar.

"Now go, the both of you," she told them, swatting their behinds. "Hurry and try to save your precious horde. Fight like you have never fought before! The bitch-goddess commands it!

"My Raiders thirst for your blood!"

She watched, then, as they ran off toward camp, childlike in their acceptance of her orders...neither fully realizing the catastrophe they were racing into. Neither knowing that the other was innocent of all blame in the death of their leader, though they were guilty of one terrible, mutual mistake.

Bringing her, the goddess of horror and devastation, the goddess of the Apocalypse, into the bosom of their horde.

Laughing, she turned and headed off across the waste, already laying out the next deadly scheme in her wicked toad of a mind.

THE CREATURE FLOATING above the table looked like a mangled lump of gray flesh wrapped in pulsing pink veins. Flaps of skin fluttered over ragged blowholes as the thing breathed, and tiny white worms like maggots crawled over its glistening mass.

"It doesn't look like much, does it?" Punji stood at one end of the table, operating the projection system. "But watch what happens if you get close enough to trigger it."

He clicked a button on the remote, and the lump of flesh suddenly leaped up and transformed, expanding rapidly into a threatening monstrosity. The four-armed, six-legged thing looked as if it had been carved from black barbed wire and gristle, all spindly and spiked. Standing at its full height, it was taller than anyone in the room—so tall, its head disappeared above the ceiling.

"So that's a Caul." Tork shook his head in wonder.

"It isn't, actually," said Punji. "It's one of their little

helpers, the ones they send out to do their dirty work for them."

As the creature beat its wiry chest and shrieked, Tork scowled. "It looks like a Caul to me," he said. "Like a walking nightmare."

"Well, it isn't," snapped Punji. "It's what we call a *Malignance*, though we have no idea what its people call themselves."

"A Malignance." Angar snorted. "Doesn't look so nasty to me."

"Spoken like someone who's never met one," said Punji. "That thing will tear through you and a hundred like you in a matter of minutes."

"And you're much more likely to face one of *those* than a Caul," added Gauge, who was sitting at a desk across the room. "Advance scouts are usually those or something like them."

"Meaning one of the other hundreds of conquered species that act as collaborators." Punji clicked the remote, and the Malignance disappeared. It was replaced by an image of something that looked like a giant cockroach mounted with s bayonets. That went away, then, and a plant-thing took its place, thrashing thorny vines like emerald bullwhips. "Any of these could be the enemy, or multiple ones working together. We just have no way of knowing what will show up."

"Then how the shang can we be ready for them?" asked Tork.

"You just have to be ready for *all* of them," said Gauge. "Or for something else we don't even *know* about yet."

"Wait," said Angar. "In the simulation, we saw what was happening on Io. The alien ship, the destruction of the dome. Can't you *see* whatever's down there? With your *science?*"

"The simulation didn't necessarily reflect what was happening on the ground," explained Gauge. "It was a guess, based on the limited telemetry we received before Io Station went dark."

"For all we know, the dome's intact," said Punji. "But don't get your hopes up, barbarians."

"The scout will have been there for more than 48 hours by the time we arrive," said Gauge. "It could have done a great deal of damage in that much time."

"Tell me something," said Tork. "Do we really think we have a *chance* against this scout, whatever it is? Or against the Caul? Because it doesn't *sound* like you *think* we do."

Punji ruffled his petals and wriggled his nozzle. "You ask a lot of *questions* for a couple of *barbarians*, you know that? I thought you'd just be happy for a chance to chop something up!"

"Don't your *other* people ask questions?" said Angar, taking Tork's side for a change. "Don't *they* deserve answers before they march off into battle?"

"You're really getting me steamed," snarled Punji. "Do you *want* me to remote-control your *mouth* shut?"

Gauge cleared his throat loudly. "We don't know." He got up from the desk and walked over to the table. "How's that for an answer to your question? We don't *know* if we have a chance."

Tork and Angar exchanged a look.

"This *ship* is special." Gauge spread his arms to take in the *Hellcyon*. "The *crew* is special. *You* and *your* people are special. I, personally, think that gives us a shot...but I don't know anything for sure. Maybe everything *is* lost already.

"But I'll be *damned* if I give up the fight before it *begins*."

With that, Gauge looked at each of them in turn. Tork could feel the passionate spirit radiating from him, inspiring in its power. It was enough to motivate even a simple barbarian, though the war was not his own, and the idea of self-sacrifice was not one he embraced on behalf of this ship of strangers.

"All right then," Gauge said at last. "I vote you study some more Caul collaborators and hit the hay early. Tomorrow will be a *hell* of a busy day." He patted Tork on the shoulder, did the same for Angar, and walked out of the conference room.

The door slid shut behind him, leaving Tork and Angar staring at the spot where he'd been.

"How long have you been with him?" Angar asked Punji. "How long has he been your lord?"

Punji snorted loudly, blowing glittery pollen all over the place. "Never! I *have* no *lord!*" He snickered, his white-flecked indigo petals jittering. "But, yes, I've served with him for a *few* years now. Ever since my own people were all but *wiped out* by the Caul."

"A few years?" said Tork.

"Forty, if you must know," snapped Punji. "And no, he wasn't always like this, if that's what you're getting at."

"He wasn't?" Angar narrowed his eyes.

"No," said Punji. "He was *much* more intense." Then, laughing some more, he played the remote, and the image over the table changed. This time, it showed something like a rhinoceros walking on two legs, with an open belly disgorging a swarm of black locust-like creatures. "And *this* is a Brevari, which is *also* quite intense when it's tearing your guts out with that snout-mounted horn."

TORK WENT in search of Angar that night and found him in the prow of the ship. He just stood there in his straps and scabbards with his hands folded behind his back, staring out through the glowing red eyes of the death's head skull.

He didn't even turn or acknowledge Tork's presence, just went on staring. He was like a statue, a stolid figure facing the onrushing starscape and the uncertain future it promised.

Tork was tempted to walk away, to leave him to his own thoughts—but things had to be said. Preparations were done for the day, the mission was just a few hours away, and he might not get another chance to speak his mind.

Though it might not make a difference, anyway.

Tork stepped up beside Angar and cleared his throat. "Are you ready for tomorrow?"

Angar didn't look at him. "Are *you* ready?"

"Maybe," said Tork. "It'll be a fight like no other, that's for sure."

"They're all the same," said Angar. "Kill or be killed."

"In space suits on another planet." Tork raised an eyebrow. "Not so much the same, after all."

Angar drew a deep breath and let it out slowly. "Why did you come here, Tork? What do you want from me?" He sounded highly annoyed.

Though Tork had come in peace, he suddenly wanted to club him over the head. Maybe he shouldn't have gone to see him after all; maybe his task was hopeless.

But he decided he had to try. "I want to know if we can do it," he said.

"Do what?" growled Angar.

"Work together." Tork turned to face him full on. "*Fight* together."

Angar smirked in the crimson light.

"Will you have my back on the battlefield?" asked Tork. "That's what I need to know."

Angar shot him a sideways look. "That's not the question you should be asking."

Tork frowned. "Then what is?"

"Why do you think you *need* me to have your back?" Angar chuckled. "Is it because you don't think you can *handle* this fight?"

"No, that's not—"

"Are you *scared?*" Angar laughed again. "Are you *frightened* of the big, bad bug people or plant people or shit-lump people?"

"I just want to know if—"

"You're a *coward*, aren't you? Just like I always *knew* you were!"

It took all the willpower Tork could muster to keep from lashing out at that instant. "No!" he shouted. "I'm no more a coward than *you* are!"

Again, Angar laughed.

"But if we're going into this shang-storm together, we *both* need to know! We need to *trust* each other, or we won't have a *chance* of saving our hordes from those *things*."

Angar sighed. "If it makes you feel better, go ahead and trust me. Expect I'll have your back. Go ahead and think that."

Tork started to say something, but Angar talked over him.

"But you should ask yourself a question, my dear old enemy." Angar faced him and leaned closer, smiling icily. "Ask yourself if it makes any sense for our *masters* to leave the kill switch on between us in the middle of a battle."

Tork scowled...but as Angar's words sank in, he realized the truth in them.

"Ask yourself, if you were the general, would you want to lose *both* your strongest fighters if *one* of them was badly wounded or killed?" Angar tipped his head to one side. "Would you *want* to let the blowback take them both out at once?"

Tork shook his head. He hated to admit it, but Angar was right.

"Now think about what *that* means to *us*." Angar reached up and poked him once in the shoulder with an index finger. "Think about what it means to *you*."

That part, Tork didn't have to be told.

Angar laughed. "But other than that, we're good, Tork. You can count on me all the way."

With that, he left the Skull, laughing all the way out the door and down the hallway.

And Tork just stood there and thought about what he'd heard and what it meant to the mission, which was just a few hours away now. He was furious because he hadn't thought of it himself.

And he was worried, because he knew it changed everything. It decreased his chances of coming back alive.

Though the same could be said, he thought, of Angar's chances.

TORK AND ANGAR *didn't say a word as they ran back to camp. They didn't talk about the death of Scalder Pacious or what the goddess Lillia had told them about who was to blame.*

They were too busy listening to the sounds of battle ringing out across the waste—the clangs of weapons, hammering of hooves, and screams of the injured and dying.

When they finally reached camp, the fight was mostly over, and the outcome clear. The Grand and Glorious Horde had been taken by surprise at their moment of greatest vulnerability. Reeling from the sudden death of their Horde Lord, they had been completely unprepared for the onrushing army of Raiders.

Many of the Horde's warriors were dead or wounded on the ground. Women and children scattered in terror, only to be rounded up by spear-toting horsemen. Tents and huts were burning, and animals were running wild into the waste.

The Grand and Glorious Horde had been routed. What had been the greatest force to roam the wastes in generations had descended into ruin and madness.

But Angar and Tork didn't let that stop them from making a last stand. They fought valiantly, grabbing weapons from the fallen and using them against the enemy with ferocious abandon. They brought down many a horse, slaughtered many a rider, and battled like demons to defend the Horde's last remnants.

Soaked in blood and covered with gore, they hacked and smashed and chopped and ripped through the enemy, roaring as they claimed brutal revenge against the attackers.

But in the end, something happened for the first time in their adult lives. Something happened that they never would have dreamed was possible.

They were defeated.

Sheer numbers overwhelmed them, pressing them down into the churned and blood-drenched dust. The Raiders chained, shackled, and muzzled them, strapping them to the back of a wagon with other survivors.

"You are now slaves!" proclaimed the leader of the enemy, a grinning man with long, blond hair like Tork's. "The days of your freedom are over! You are our property and will be sold, put to work, or destroyed as we see fit."

From his place behind the wagon, Tork blinked away the blood running into his eyes. He barely took notice of the Raider's words as they flowed over him. There was someone else he hated even more, someone he blamed for everything.

Someone he wanted to kill.

It was the same for Angar as he looked over at his lifelong friend. If his glare had been the blade of a broadsword, he would have hacked Tork into pieces right there and then, and damn the consequences.

When the leader of the Raiders was done gloating and

threatening, he and his people headed out across the waste with their parade of prisoners in tow. The heavens opened up then, sending down a deluge to soak and hobble them, turning the ground beneath them into mud. People fell in their traces and were dragged if they couldn't get up. The slightest move by one survivor to help another was rewarded with the crack of a barbed whip.

Angar and Tork never flagged or missed a step. They strode forward with shoulders squared, walking into whatever terrible future awaited them...dreaming of just one thing, the same thing between them.

Dreaming of the moment when they could get their hands around each other's throats and squeeze.

PART III

INFERNO

Hours later, the *Hellcyon* lurched out of Rip Space with more shuddering than usual, even as the crew in the Cortex fought to stabilize her.

"Jupiter's pulling us in too fast!" Lt. Jelani's fingers wove across the holographic helm controls with practiced ease, as if she were under no pressure at all. "Increasing power to the thrusters. Plotting an orbit around Io."

Tork and Angar watched from wall-mounted jumpseats in the back of the room. They'd learned better than to stay standing in the Cortex during Rip travel.

"Course set and locked," said Jelani. "Activating thrusters and starting final approach."

As she said it, Tork felt the ship bump into its new path and saw the starfield jolt beyond the see-through floor and ceiling. Io hung like a ball of yellow clay against the rainbow-striped backdrop of Jupiter, looking tiny, distant, and quiet—not at all like the site of an impending battle.

"All is well," said Jelani. "We will achieve Io orbit in approximately seventeen minutes."

"Good." Gauge was up out of his chair, pacing the floor from station to station. "Immediate threats?"

Lt. Skeezik was fully focused on the dozen holoscreens floating around him. "None detectable, sir, but we are watching closely for the faintest flicker."

"Keep at it." Gauge looked back at Tork and Angar and nodded. "You two. It's time."

Tork smacked the armrest button that released his harness and pushed up out of the jumpseat. Angar did the same.

"Report to the launch bay and suit up," said Gauge. "Your teams will be waiting there for you."

"On our way." Tork headed for the door, with Angar close behind.

"And remember, everything's riding on this," said Gauge. "Every*one*. The entire Annihilation Alliance. Every survivor of the Caul conquest of our galaxy. Today is either the start of our last chance or the end of all hope."

"Yes," said Angar. "We will do our best."

"We will *crush* anyone who gets in our way!" shouted Tork. "We promise you that!"

"Be sure you do," said Gauge. "For all our sakes."

A SPEEDING CART nearly took out Tork as he entered the busy launch bay. The speed of its passage brushed him back so fast, he nearly knocked over Angar in turn.

Angar caught him by the shoulder, though, and kept

him on his feet. "Easy does it," he said. "Don't get yourself hurt before you even leave the ship." The chuckle that followed was condescending and hate-laced as always.

Tork pushed away and continued forward with more care. Vehicles and people caromed everywhere, making it a challenge to cross the room without another collision.

The bay was even crazier and more crowded than usual, with uniformed crewmembers running in all directions, carrying all manner of equipment. Others swarmed around a group of craft lined up at the bay doors—six of them, compact and needle-nosed, with sleek silver bodies and bubble-canopied cockpits.

Tork guessed what they were for and wished they were bigger. Flying in such a cramped ship might not be his ideal way of getting to the surface of Io.

Not to mention, flying a spaceship was one thing his hosts had neglected to teach him how to do.

"Over there." Angar pointed at the closest ship, where Major Schist was waving for their attention. "My supposed second-in-command is calling."

Tork's second was there, too, at Schist's side—a creature that looked like a cross between a spider and a snake. It was called a Sisslak, and her name was Valla Voss.

As the barbarians approached, Schist stood at attention and fired off a crisp forehead salute in Angar's direction. "Sir." His crystalline body glowed blue for the moment, indicating a state of calm. "We're ready for you."

"Sssame with your team, sssir." Valla bowed her black spidery head at Tork. "Ssstanding by for ordersss."

Tork nodded, feeling off balance. He was used to

barking out commands to the horde back home, but he was out of his element here.

Angar, on the other hand, seemed fine with it. "Prepare to launch," he told Schist. "Do it!"

Schist's glow shifted pink, expressing annoyance. "By that, do you mean to help you suit up, run a pre-flight check on the skiff, load your weapons, get the rest of the team boarded, and signal all clear to flight control?"

Angar looked confused for a second, then nodded. "Yes, yes, of course. All that."

Valla tapped Tork on the shoulder and lowered her voice. "Would you like me to do the sssame, sssir?"

"Sure." Tork smiled. "Why the shang not?"

Just then, Gauge's voice boomed over the speakers. "Five minutes until we make orbit. Io teams, you will launch in five."

Valla clicked her glossy black mandibles twice. "We'd better get rolling. Lotsss to do in five minutesss."

She was right...and also the perfect one to get it all done. Between her eight legs, clawed feet, and prehensile tail, Valla was able to handle multiple tasks at once.

Though Major Schist lacked the extra legs, feet, and tail, he made up for it with efficiency and flair. He got Angar into his armored spacesuit in nothing flat, ran the pre-flight checklist in a flash, loaded Angar's weapons in the hold, and got his team boarded, two per skiff, without delay...with one exception.

Angar hesitated, looking into the cramped cockpit, even as Gauge spoke over the loudspeaker again. "We are at T-minus one minute and counting! Launch in one minute, people!"

"We weren't trained for this," muttered Angar.

"Not a problem," said Schist. "Skiff runs on autopilot, and I'll be at the controls. You can just sit back and leave the driving to me."

"Is there a bigger one?" asked Angar.

Schist reddened. The clock was counting down, and launch was imminent. "No, but you'll be fine. Skiffs are pretty comfortable once you get inside."

Angar bunched his fists, intending to resist further— then got distracted by something fluttering around him. Scowling, he swatted at it, then stopped when he realized what it was.

A butterfly.

Just then, he heard someone clearing her throat behind him and turned to see Quinza there, smiling and waving.

"Hello, Angar." The butterfly returned to its perch among the many on her head, settling gently into place. "I just came to wish you good luck."

Angar instantly felt calmer. "Thanks." He nodded.

"Hey, Horde Lord!" shouted Schist. "Hurry up and get in! We've got to go!"

"I won't keep you." Quinza seemed to understand without being told. "Just remember, wherever you are, you can always go to your happy place in your mind."

Angar relaxed further. "I'll try my best. Thanks for reminding me."

"So you've found your happy place, then? Other than a battlefield?" asked Quinza. "You know where it is?"

"Maybe." Angar managed a smile of his own. "I think maybe I do."

"That's good," said Quinza. "Then I'll see you when you

get back. Take care." She blew him a kiss and ran off, the butterflies fluttering in the breeze of her walk as she went.

He watched her for one moment more. Then, without another word, he climbed into the rear seat, armor and all, and squeezed himself into place.

"So you got the blessing of the Pale Lady? The Goddess Acquiesce?" Schist nodded approvingly. "Congratulations. Maybe we'll survive this nightmare after all."

Angar looked where he'd last seen Quinza, but she was gone.

Tork, meanwhile, hesitated long enough to see Angar do the deed, then got into his own skiff. Schist had lied; it wasn't comfortable at all. If anything, it made him feel claustrophobic.

And it didn't get any better when Valla the spider-headed, spider-legged boa constrictor clambered into the seat in front of him.

"T-minus thirty seconds," said Gauge over the speakers.

"Buckle up!" Valla turned, deftly wrapped the seat harness around him, and clicked the buckle home over his chest. Then, she returned to facing front and threw a switch on the control panel that made the canopy quickly slide shut over the cockpit. "The fun'sss about to begin."

As they sat there in the skiff, Tork found himself counting backward, getting more nervous with each passing second. It was a new feeling to him, this nervousness in the face of the unknown, something he'd never felt back home on Earth. Even his dealings with the Blacksmiths on Earth had been somewhat predictable, likely to occur within certain parameters—but today, he was truly going off into the unknown.

He would have denied it with his dying breath, but he was afraid—and hated himself for feeling that way.

Then, the countdown ended, and even the fear was forgotten.

"T-minus ten seconds!" said Gauge.

The bay doors swung open, revealing the yellow orb of Io racing closer, Jupiter's red spot looming behind it.

Tork looked left, at the next skiff in line, and saw Angar looking back at him. He thought he saw a flicker of worry cross Angar's face—and then Angar grinned and winked.

"Launch in five...four...three..." said Gauge.

"Hang onto your cookiesss, bosss!" said Valla as she flicked switches and pressed buttons. The skiff started to vibrate, and its engines rumbled with rising intensity.

"Two...one!" said Gauge. "Launch! And may all the lost souls of the galaxy be with you!"

"Our prey awaitsss!" shouted Valla, and then she punched a red button in the middle of the console. "Let'sss go get 'em!"

With that, the rumbling of the engines became a thunderous roar. The skiff leaped forward, shooting out of the launch bay and into the starry darkness of space.

FLYING to Io in the skiff wasn't anything like flying in the simulation had been.

At first, Angar *hated* it. He didn't like being cooped up in the cockpit, hardly able to move. The skiff's dizzying maneuvers stressed his body, churning his guts as he raced toward the pale, yellow moon with the giant planet behind it. Most of all, he hated not having control over where he was going and how he was getting there.

But soon enough, he changed his mind. As Schist guided the skiff closer to Io, and the moon's surface leaped toward him in sharp detail, Angar got lost in the beauty of that alien scenery. Seeing it in person was very different from seeing it in a computer simulation, and the fact that he was physically *there* made it all the more exciting.

The skiff skimmed over vast ranges of yellow and rust mountains, working its way lower with each passing mile.

Plumes of smoke streamed up from dark craters, gray columns curling up on all sides as the skiff banked and swam in between them. In the distance, a blast of fiery gas and lava surged into the sky, marking the eruption of one of Io's multitude of volcanoes.

Still, the skiff dipped lower, threading its way through the fuming, heaving landscape. Soon, he'd set foot down there, stepping on the surface of another world for the first time...and the thought of that was enough to make the jaded warrior experience something else for what might also have been the first time.

A sense of wonder.

Not that anyone had much time for that today. "There's an unusual amount of seismic activity." Schist keyed commands into the console and punched a glowing green button. "Transmitting sensor data back to the *Hellcyon* now."

"Size-mick?" Angar frowned.

"Instability in the ground," said Schist. "It tells us when earthquakes or volcanic eruptions are likely."

As if in response, a spire of fiery gas shot out of a vent in their path, forcing Schist to veer the skiff hard to port. They missed the flaming spire, but Angar swore he could feel the heat of it through the skin of the skiff.

As they cleared that obstacle, the dome of Io Station came into view, glinting through the cleft between two high yellow ridges.

"There it is." Crystalline head glowing orange, Schist hit a series of controls across the console, and static crackled over the speakers. "Io Station, come in. This is

Hellcyon skiff A-7, over." He paused then, listening, but the static didn't change. "Io Station, this is Major Lavish Schist, over."

Still, there was nothing but static.

"Why aren't you using the thinklink?" asked Angar.

"The station crew aren't equipped with thinklink," said Schist. "We need to stick with old-fashioned radio to reach them. Understand?"

"Sure," said Angar.

Schist went back to putting out the call. "Io Station, please respond, over." Again, he waited through the static. "Nothing."

"All dead?" asked Angar.

"Not necessarily." Schist tried again as the dome grew larger up ahead. Again, no one answered his call. "There are many possible explanations."

Angar grunted. "We should expect the worst. Be ready for anything."

"Absolutely, given the circumstances," said Schist.

As the dome got bigger, Schist got busier, running scans and checking readouts while flying the skiff with the autopilot. Angar just kept watching over his shoulder, looking for signs of attack or the battle to come.

But none were yet visible. If the scout had breached the dome, whatever havoc it had wrought was well concealed.

Schist switched off the radio mic, and Angar heard him in his mind through the thinklink. "Attention, skiffs, this is squad leader. Let's swoop in for a closer look. All weapons armed and ready."

~

"ROGER THAT, SSSQUAD LEADER," Valla said with her thoughts. "Armed and ready."

Tork's stomach lurched as the skiff accelerated suddenly, bolting after Schist and Angar's craft. Looking to either side from the bubble canopy, he saw the rest of the squad gliding alongside them, two ships on his left and two on his right.

"Form up!" Valla said via thinklink, and they did just that, slipping into a single-file formation. "Let's go, people!"

The dome loomed, and Angar's skiff shot toward it. Valla followed, with the other four close behind.

The distance shrank fast, and Tork caught himself jittering nervously. Io Station was the only base on that moon, so the chances of the interloper being there were pretty good. The thought of clashing with it was worrisome...and also exciting. It had been too long since his last bloody conflict, and he wanted to try out his new Blacksmith-built weapons.

"Take a good look on the first passs, bosss," Valla told him. "It might be the only one we get."

"I will." Tork sat straighter, gaze fixed on the approaching dome. From where they were, it looked intact, not torn asunder as it had appeared in the simulation.

As they flew closer, he saw the structures under the dome looked undamaged, too. The yellow stone buildings with their many windows and solar panels looked as if they'd just been freshly erected.

But as they soared closer still, Schist pointed out something over thinklink. "I don't see any lights, do you?"

Valla flew up alongside him. "Roger that, Major. No visible power consssumption."

"That's good news," said someone in another skiff behind them—a voice in Tork's head that he recognized as belonging to an ironclad creature called Rerox Demagorn. "Maybe the coms loss was due to a power failure, and we've got warm bodies down there after all.

"Maybe." Valla closed the thinklink channel with the click of a mandible and said the rest for Tork's benefit. "Or the Caul ssscout isss the only warm body we're gonna find after all this time."

Tork nodded. "Unless they're holding prisoners to use against us."

"Oh, bosss." Valla made a chattering sound he thought might be laughter. "The Caul don't *take* pris-onersss."

On they flew, banking along the curve of the great dome in the wake of Schist and Angar's skiff. The whole time, Tork never took his eyes off the buildings in the dome, and he never saw a flicker of movement or artificial light other than that coming from the skiffs' reflections on the polished surface.

"No life signs," said Schist over thinklink.

Valla reopened the link to reply. "Which meansss noth-ing. We know the Caul and their agentsss can interfere with sssensssor accuracy."

"No sign of the scout ship, either," said Schist. "We need to split up."

Valla twisted her head around to look at Tork. "Three

teamsss in the dome to hunt the pilot, three teamsss to ssseek the ssscout ship?"

Tork frowned. "Shouldn't we *all* be hunting the pilot at once?"

"Disabling the ship's a priority," said Schist. "Before the pilot trips its beacon and summons the fleet."

"Which for sssome reassson, it hasssn't done yet," said Valla.

"Fine," said Tork. "Send *one* team after the ship and the rest after the invader."

"Agreed," Angar said over the link. "And that one team should be *mine*, Tork."

"You and I need to stay together," said Tork. "To face this monster with *all* our combined power."

"Clearly, that ship is just as much of a threat!" snapped Angar. "And it's probably booby-trapped as well. Or maybe there's someone else aboard to defend it. Do you really want to send a Blacksmith without my *killer instinct* to go after it?"

Tork didn't like the idea at all. He was sure Angar was maneuvering for reasons he couldn't fathom at the moment, planning another step in whatever conquest he had in mind. Was it just because he wanted Tork out of the way, and having him face the Caul pilot would be the surest way of doing that?

"I think *I* should go after the ship," said Tork.

Angar snorted. "And you expect *me* to lead the teams after the pilot?"

"Unless you're not up to the challenge," said Tork.

"All right." Angar sighed. "Have it your way. You and your second in command go ahead and find the scout ship. Everyone else, come with me."

"Good luck," said Tork. "And try not to get hurt too bad, all right? I don't want the *blowback* kicking my ass because *you* keep getting *smashed up.*"

"I wouldn't worry about blowback," said Angar. "You already know what I think about it in *this* situation."

Tork did, but he didn't get the chance to say anything else about it. Angar's skiff dropped suddenly, followed by the other skiffs...except one. Tork's maintained its altitude and sailed on ahead, clearing the dome and zooming into a range of volcanic hills venting pillars of fire.

"I guesss we're on our own," said Valla. "But it'sss for the bessst. Your buddy would only ssslow usss down."

"You think so?" Tork stared out of the cockpit, wondering if he'd done the right thing—or played right into Angar's hands. Had Angar *wanted* him to do the opposite of what his first instinct had dictated?

"I *know* ssso." Valla steered the skiff around the fiery plumes with style, swooping gracefully as a bird gliding between upswept thermals back home. "You sssee, I have *amazing* luck. Whatever choiccce I make, it'sss alwaysss the right one."

"That's good to know," said Tork, though he wasn't convinced.

"Do you want to know *how* good my luck is?" Valla hammered on a keyboard built into the console, punched some buttons, and a glowing red grid appeared in midair between her and the front glass of the cockpit. "Check *thiss* out." Another rattle of keys, and a ring of blinking red dots appeared in the top right corner of the grid.

Tork frowned. "What is it?"

"That Caul ssscout ship we expected to find on the ground? It's *airborne.*" Valla clacked her mandibles and rattled her reptilian tail. "And it's *seven* ships, not *one*. And they're headed *this way.*"

27

As the dome's airlock irised open, Angar shifted his grip on his broadsword, getting ready for anything that might leap out at him.

But nothing did.

When Schist shone his wrist-mounted flashlight into the space beyond the door, Angar saw it was empty. No alien pilot waited to pounce, and no visible traps could be seen.

"All clear." Schist moved to step in first, but Angar caught him by the shoulder and pushed ahead, asserting his leadership.

The lock was barely big enough to fit the full group of ten. Fortunately, they wouldn't be in there long; the power might be out elsewhere in the dome, but the airlock equipment was working just fine.

The room rumbled, the outer door irised shut, and a wall-mounted digital timer counted down from 30. When the blinking red digits reached 00:00, the rumbling stopped, and a circular door opposite the door to the outside opened with the same iris pattern that the first door had used.

As Angar stepped through with his broadsword at the ready, a city of yellow stone and glass buildings sprawled before him.

"All dark." Schist looked around. "All quiet."

He removed his helmet then, hanging it from a hook on his belt, and everyone else did the same. They took turns breathing deep, testing the air...nodding with satisfaction that the atmosphere inside the dome was breathable.

Then, as a group, they started forward.

"Something is definitely blocking our sensors," said Rerox Demagorn. His ironclad body banged and clanked as he walked behind Angar and Schist. "A kind of steady interference wave, from what I can tell."

"Nothing like going in blind," said another team member, a young woman named Bastis Candra. "Not that any of this seems the *slightest* bit ominous."

"Shut up and focus on your surroundings," snapped Angar. "*Sensors* are no match for *senses.*"

Holding tight to his broadsword, keenly aware of the battle axe clamped to his back and the rifle on his left hip, he proceeded forward along the hard-packed yellow street. He wasn't sure what he was looking for, any more than the rest of them were, but he was ready to face it with all the power at his command.

As he walked past the nearest yellow building, he squinted at the windows and wondered if anyone was watching from inside. His gut told him to keep going, so he did...though he worried his gut could be as wrong as the sensors.

His heart hammered, and his spine tingled. The thought of what he was doing and the danger he faced was like something out of a strange and thrilling dream.

"Maybe we should call out," said Candra. "See if anyone answers."

"No," said Angar. "If anyone's here, they'll come to us."

He led the team further into the station, all with weapons at the ready. His confidence in these novices was rock-bottom, though his faith in his own skills could not be shaken. He planned to confront any situation that came his way with irresistible force.

"What about this one?" Schist pointed at the next building, a low structure with bands of tinted windows all the way around.

Again, Angar did not feel the familiar pressure of being watched. "No." He slashed his sword from side to side for emphasis. "Not there."

Suddenly, then, a terrible shriek pierced the air, coming from the direction of the next building in line. A clatter of guns followed as the team swung their rifles as one toward that sound.

Schist's crystalline head glowed fiery red. "There!" He planted the butt of the rifle against his shoulder and aimed the barrel at the building from which the scream had originated.

Angar stopped and took in the details. The building was narrow, four stories tall, rust-colored, and window-less, with an arched black door on the side facing the street.

It was so closed in, he thought. So *wrong*.

"Keep going." Sword in hand, he continued past the windowless building, following the street along the curve of the dome.

Another shriek, louder than the first, erupted from that same building as he left it behind.

"Horde Lord," said Schist as he hurried along beside him. "Shouldn't we follow the screams?"

"Go ahead." Angar kept walking. "*I* won't, but *you* can."

Schist frowned and looked back but stayed with him. The rest of the team did the same, though there was some muttering among them.

Followed by another shriek from the same place.

"Horde Lord," said Schist.

Suddenly, Angar stopped and stared at a towering structure up ahead—a needle-nosed steeple, the highest building under the dome.

"What is it?" asked Schist.

Angar's answer was to jog toward the base of that steeple, sword at the ready. He'd glimpsed movement there, a flicker of reflected light—the first he'd seen since leaving the airlock.

As he drew closer, a bulky figure charged out of a door in the base and headed right for him. He was huge, over seven feet tall, heavily muscled, and wore a helmet with great upswept horns like those of a bull. Patterns of light danced over his gleaming armor, and his massive axe threw sparks as it cleaved the air.

The onrushing warrior looked as if he could lay waste to the team from the *Hellcyon* a dozen times over. His

bestial roar was the universal language of furious challenge, a proclamation of animal dominance.

Grinning, Angar thumbed the glowing red stud on the
hilt of his sword, activating its electrical field. Then,
swinging the crackling, gleaming sword, he broke into a
full-tilt run to meet that challenge.

28

"I'M GONNA VEER OFF, bosss! We gotta get outta the way of those shipsss, right?" Before Tork could answer, Valla wrenched the joystick to one side, and the skiff banked hard in that direction.

Tork just glowered, watching as geysers of flaming gas and molten rock leaped up in the skiff's path. Valla steered around them with consummate skill, swooping from one to the other without even brushing a single superheated stream.

"Ssso much for the sssingle ship in the original telemetry." Valla sounded annoyed as she threaded the field of fiery columns. "How did they misss the other sssix ssspacecraft?"

The skiff had to flip on its side to squeeze between two close-set jets of flame that suddenly sprang to life. Tork held his breath, convinced the little ship wouldn't clear the channel...but it did.

"We sure could use some of the other ssskiffsss right

now," said Valla. "Want me to call them back out from the dome?"

Tork thought fast, assessing the situation. He was heading for enemy forces that unexpectedly outnumbered him by a wide margin. His allies in the dome were in their path and didn't suspect the size of the attack group.

His instinct was to go at them head-on, but another course of action might be more critical to the big picture.

"Can we get new pictures and send a warning?" he asked. "Notify the *Hellcyon* and the teams in the dome?"

"As long as we ssstay out of *their* sssensssor range." Valla typed away on the control panel and twisted the joystick, bringing the skiff around. "I'll do my bessst to masssk our heat sssignature among the active volcanic ventsss."

"Okay." Tork watched her legs and tail dance over the panel, touching seemingly every control at least once every thirty seconds. The skiff bumped and swam through the hazy atmosphere, missing one fiery geyser after another.

Finally, through the veil of smoke and flame, Tork glimpsed the enemy squad. He counted six streamlined white ships, their size reduced with distance, flying in a loose circular formation.

"I see them," he said. "Six, at least. Can you get what we need from here?"

"The volcanic haze is reducing the effectiveness of our cameras and sssenssssors," she said. "We need to get clossser."

She slid the skiff further across the field of vents,

dropping back a little in the process. The Caul ships proceeded on course, taking no notice.

"Let'sss make this quick, we're awfully close." Valla worked the controls, and there were clicking sounds in the cockpit. "Photos are coming in fine. Zooming in—got it. Sssenssor data is ssstill sssparsssse, though."

Tork squinted into the haze, picking out the bone-white craft. "How many ships do you count, Valla?"

"Sssix," she said, manipulating keys and buttons on the console.

"But shouldn't there be seven?"

"Sssensssors did show sssseven at first," said Valla. "But they've been unreliable. Maybe it was a glitch or ghost in the sssysssstem."

"Or maybe it moved out of range," said Tork. "Maybe it spotted us and..."

A sudden impact rocked the skiff, knocking his head against the glass. As Valla struggled with the controls, he peered out the window on one side, just in time to see an enemy ship diving past, white with black and yellow stripes on its wings.

Then, he looked out the window on the other side and saw the remaining six ships racing toward the skiff. Performing secret reconnaissance was no longer an option.

The Caul's entire squad was zooming straight for them.

CLANG! KZZZZ!

Angar's electrified sword crashed into the blade of the horn-helmeted warrior's axe with staggering force. As the vibrations from the impact traveled up his arm, Angar clenched his teeth and grinned. *Finally*, he was doing what he loved most, battling a savage opponent in all-out combat for the highest stakes.

The bull-horned warrior strained to press him back and down, to no avail. Angar was a head smaller and not as bulked-up, but his strength and fortitude were the equal of this monstrous foe.

With a surge of effort, Angar broke the clinch, pivoted, and swept his broadsword around for a high-slashing strike. Roaring, the warrior caught it with the axe and braced it overhead. Though the axe wasn't electrically charged like Angar's, it was so solidly made that it held the sword in check without faltering.

CLANG! KZZZZ!

As they stood there like that, deadlocked, Angar got his first good look at the enemy's face. He'd expected something alien and horrible, worthy of the stories he'd heard about the vicious Caul and their allies.

Instead, he saw something familiar.

The helmet covered the top and sides of the warrior's head, and a protective, ridged faceplate extended midway down the front. It left the lower half of the face uncovered, though, revealing a mouth and chin that appeared to be human. The eyes, visible through holes in the faceplate, looked human as well...and green.

What in Yorg's name?

Even without any formal knowledge of alien life and its evolution, Angar was shocked that a Caul overlord or servant would have a face and body that were remotely human. On the other hand, he was happy enough to have an opponent who provided a challenge—one who wasn't part of a damn simulation aboard the *Hellcyon*.

"Rarrgh!" The warrior heaved off Angar's sword and sent him stumbling back a step, then pressed the attack with an axe slash aimed at his chest.

The giant blade sliced through the breastplate of Angar's armor, barely missing his chest underneath. Though Angar still believed the Blacksmiths had switched off the blowback link before things had gotten too dangerous, he wondered if Tork, wherever he was, had felt the whisper of the sharp edge skimming through his own chest hair.

Before the backswing, Angar hacked the edge of his sword at the warrior's side, but it bounced off the glowing armor without doing any damage.

Angar barely got the sword up in time to deflect the latest sweep of the axe. Sparks flew as the two blades met with titanic force, smashing together in a collision that would have shattered lesser weapons.

CLANG! KZZZZ!

Again and again, the blades clashed, and the men wielding them struggled. No flash of victory ever lasted long; when one seized the advantage, the other quickly snatched it away.

CLANG! CLANG! CLANG! KZZZZ!

Meanwhile, Angar's team encircled them with rifles raised, waiting for a clear shot to fire. None of them were sharpshooters, so they weren't taking any chances; Angar knew he'd have to be well clear before they'd risk firing.

Not that Angar was in a hurry for them to gun down his foe. As much fun as he was having, they could take their time picking a shot.

Soon enough, he realized they wouldn't be taking that shot at all. Angar heard shouts and running footsteps, and his team swung their weapons away from the one-on-one clash.

Peering past the warrior between swings of the axe and sword, he saw the reason for his team's change of focus. A dozen more warriors were charging out of surrounding buildings and alleys, each armored and carrying their own fearsome weaponry.

And they were heading directly for the circle of inexperienced crewmen who'd probably never killed anything bigger than a bug in their lives.

BEAMS of deadly white energy strafed the hazy sky around the skiff as the cannons of the six enemy ships lit up in unison.

"Hang on!" Valla bobbed the skiff from side to side, dodging the incoming beams as best she could. "Things are about to get *choppy* up here."

The skiff took a hit that spun it into an open area, free of volcanic geysers. As Valla kicked on the thrusters and stopped the spin, Tork looked out the cockpit and saw the seventh ship darting toward them, the one with the black and yellow stripes on its wings, making another solo run.

"Wait till the last second and drop," said Tork.

"I've got a better idea." Valla flipped the cover off a bright red button on the joystick. "It's called, 'shoot the bassstard.'"

When she squeezed the button with one of her talons, the skiff shook with chattering force. Tork saw slugs of blazing matter blast out of the forward guns, streaking toward the enemy ship.

As Tork watched, several of the slugs pounded the bone-white fuselage of the ship, staggering its approach. Another round caught it in the nose, flipping it end over end out of the attack lane.

But then, the other six ships barged back into the picture, hurtling up in an X formation. Again, their guns flared to life.

"It'sss getting *ugly.*" Valla squeezed off rounds of flaming slugs at the X formation, crossing fire with the enemy's volley of energy beams. "We're outnumbered and outgunned. Nothing good can come of thisss."

Tork held tight as the skiff bucked hard. "Forget the drop." He glared past Valla at the view of the oncoming ships from the front window. "Hit them head on. Take out the ship in the middle of the X."

Just as he said it, a direct hit blitzed the cockpit from behind. The rogue seventh ship was responsible, zipping past and ducking away when the damage was done.

The cockpit shed panes of reinforced glass, and waves of intense heat washed in. Sweat rolled down Tork's face inside the helmet, and he had no way to brush it aside.

"Maybe we should run," said Valla. "Sssee if we can lose them amid the volcanic activity."

"No!" snapped Tork. "Drive right through the middle of their formation!"

"*Then* what?" asked Valla.

"Leave it to me!" Tork unsnapped the buckles of his harness and peeled aside the straps. "Now *go!*"

"Yesss, sssir!" Valla didn't sound so certain as she

punched buttons on the panel and worked the joystick. "Full ssspeed ahead."

As the skiff charged forward, Tork smashed out the remaining glass in the cockpit frame around him, clearing it with his elbow. Then, he rose from his seat, reaching for his battle axe behind him. Energy beams strafing all around, he stood straight with his axe raised overhead, roaring a war cry within his helmet as the skiff barreled toward the ship in the center of the X like a giant bullseye.

ANGAR QUICKLY REALIZED his team was in trouble.

People hesitated to open fire on the warriors charging toward them. How many times had they practiced shooting at enemy forces? Yet firing weapons in a simulation was very different from using lethal force in a real-world, real-time situation.

When team members finally pulled the triggers on their burner rifles, the results were mixed. Some shots hit home, punching slugs of superheated plasma into the center masses of their enemies. But for every fallen foe, others were untouched and closing fast. The competent shooters on the team moved to take up the slack, but by then, the warriors were within throwing distance, swinging their weapons overhead.

Two things were clear at that point: Angar would have to intervene, fighting the team's opponents as well as his own...and even then, some of his rattled people wouldn't survive.

He took a breath and centered himself, gathering all the strength at his command. Meeting the gaze of the warrior straining against him, he calmly took his measure.

Then, as the wave of warriors was about to reach his team, he unleashed himself. Adrenaline blazed through his arteries, pumping fresh power into his body, and he channeled it like a raging river into the brutal work at hand.

Roaring, he lashed a booted foot into the armored shin of his foe with enough force to make it buckle. At the same time, he heaved off the axe with his broadsword, breaking the warrior's grip on it. The axe clattered to the street, and the warrior crashed down beside it.

It was the perfect moment to annihilate his foe, but other business was more pressing. Without pausing, he whirled and ran for the perimeter, aiming for the area of most urgent need.

Clearly, that was Bastis Candra, a purple-haired woman who was being double-teamed by a pair of warriors. One of them smacked the rifle out of her hands, even as the other raised his spiked mace high, about to crush her skull into butter.

Angar leaped in like a force of nature and spiked his sword through the open space below the first warrior's faceplate. Thumbing the hilt stud, he juiced the sword's power setting; he'd kept it low with his first opponent, enjoying the fight—but the time for playing was over.

Moving fast, Angar wrenched the sword free and let the warrior keel over backward. Then, in the space of a heartbeat, he hacked the sword up at the neck of the mace-wielder's armor. With the blade's power maxed, it swiftly burned its way through the armored joint and sliced into the warrior's flesh, making him scream like a child as blood sprayed everywhere.

Satisfied, Angar kicked him over and darted off to his next bout, leaving Candra to retrieve her gun and make up for her poor shooting the first time around.

"Angar!" When Schist shouted his name, Angar thought it was a call for help, and he whipped around to see where he was needed. Instead, as he quickly realized, it was a warning.

The first warrior he'd fought was back on his feet, charging him like a bull elephant. Angar went down hard, dropping his sword, blacking out as his head bounced on the street.

TORK stood ready as Valla piloted the skiff toward the enemy squadron, dodging beams of energy while staying on course for the middle ship. Steely gaze fixed on the target, he held tight to the handle of the battle axe and braced one foot against the cockpit frame. He counted down the seconds until his big move, counted down the dwindling distance between the skiff and the enemy ship.

"What do you want me to do when we get there?" asked Valla, her voice coming in loud and clear over the thinklink.

"Go after the seventh ship," he told her. "The harrier. Take it out of the mix."

"What about the other sssix?" asked Valla.

"Don't worry." Tork adjusted his grip on the axe and tensed, ready to explode into action. "I'll take care of them."

"All *sssix?*"

"I said I'll take care of them," Tork said grimly.

"Well, good luck, bosss!" said Valla as the nose of the skiff raced toward the middle ship.

"You too." Heart pounding as the thinklink connection closed, he crouched, gauging the distance, mapping his battle plan. He wondered, if he died, if Angar would die, too, because of the blowback.

Then, just as Valla veered off, he burst from the skiff, leaping across the smoky gap at the enemy craft.

He landed heavily on the nose of the middle ship, his magnetic boots grabbing the metal surface, and immediately sprinted forward along the fuselage. He knew he had to take action right away or risk being shaken by the pilot.

Unlike the skiff, there was no cockpit with a transparent canopy conveniently at hand—but a V-shaped ridge spanned the surface of the ship's disk, opaque white and perhaps significant. Without a lot of time to think it over and select a better target, he headed straight for it.

Swinging up the axe, he propelled himself in a great flying leap and came down in the bow of the V. Thumbing the glowing red stud on the weapon's handle, he powered up the axe as he swung it down at the V-shaped ridge. The electrified blade cleaved through the metallic skin without resistance, shedding sparks as it cut deep.

Howling a war cry within his helmet, he wrenched out the axe and chopped it down again. The ship wobbled, and he kept going, exposing the interior.

A few more strikes, and a figure in a black helmet and space suit leaped out, firing blasts from an energy beam weapon. Tork cut his head off with a single stroke of the crackling battle axe.

The helmet separated first, drifting off in the low gravity, revealing the severed head inside.

And Tork's eyes shot wide open in utter shock at what he saw. He'd expected some kind of fearsome alien creature gaping back at him, something outside his experience.

Instead, he saw the head of a man his age, a human male with thick red hair and a dark black beard.

Was it possible? Were human beings manning the ships of the terrible Caul?

THE SCREAMS of the bull-horned warrior snapped Angar out of the blackness. Gazing up from the street, he saw the warrior howling to the sky as plasma slugs from a Blacksmith burner rifle sizzled through the armor on his chest.

Scrambling to his feet and looking back, Angar saw Candra standing behind him with rifle raised, smoke curling from the barrel. Angar had saved her earlier, and now she'd returned the favor.

But there was no time for exchanging a word between them. Looking past her, Angar saw another team member in jeopardy, a brown-skinned young man named Ben who was besieged by a brawny warrior with a bladed fighting staff.

Grabbing his broadsword off the street, Angar charged across the battlefield. He could see Ben was injured and losing ground, using his damaged rifle to fend off the staff.

Bolting through the melee, Angar hauled back his sword and threw it, sending it spinning end over end at his target. The heavy sword crashed into the warrior's helmeted skull, kicking it back, and Angar followed up with a volley of plasma slugs from his rifle. The warrior toppled to the street, slugs cooking through the armor into his torso and thighs.

Swordless now, Angar blasted away with the gun, spraying slugs at other warriors attacking his people. Though it wasn't the kind of fighting he was used to, he admired the power and efficiency, the way it enabled him to take down opponents with great accuracy from a distance. It made him wonder, though, why the enemy warriors weren't equipped with the same weaponry.

Just as that thought occurred to him, he heard a piercing scream and whirled to face the source. Candra was the one making the noise, gaping at a terrible scene unfolding on the street before her.

The body of the warrior she'd killed moments ago was writhing on the yellow pavement, flopping and twisting like a fish on the shore. As Angar watched, the animated corpse flung itself up and violently unfolded, shedding its glistening crimson innards. Flexing and rolling, it reshaped itself, becoming a spiked monstrosity of black barbed wire and white gristle.

Angar recognized the thing instantly from his briefing aboard the *Hellcyon* on Caul allies and servants. *"Malignance."* He hissed out the name in a hateful breath as the thing's transformation continued.

Mesmerized, Candra stood there, the rifle shaking in her hands. If she didn't snap out of it soon...

"Candra, shoot it!" Angar ran toward her as he shouted, unable to use his own rifle because she was blocking his shot. "Fire! Do it now!"

A slime-drenched black hump extruded itself from the chest of the wriggling mess. As Angar ran, it puckered open, puffing a glittering mist in Candra's direction.

The cloud of mist enshrouded her. Not only didn't she pull the trigger, but she put the gun down.

"Get away!" Angar's heart hammered with desperation. "Go! Get away!"

Clamping his own rifle at his hip, he hurtled forward with arms outstretched. Whatever spell she was under, his only chance was to snatch her away.

And then there was no chance at all.

In the space of a heartbeat, a dozen slime-drenched tubules sprang from the abdomen of the gruesome Malignance and fired a barrage of projectiles at Candra. Her body jerked and jolted as they riddled it from head to foot, penetrating her armor as if it weren't there.

THUK-UK-UK-UK-UK-UK-UK

Angar stumbled to a halt, reaching for his rifle. Now he knew why the warriors weren't carrying guns.

It was because they *were* the guns.

And the rest of his team understood, as well, all at once. The sickening sound echoed in the street from all directions as the rest of the enemy fallen transformed and activated the same way.

THUK-UK-UK-UK-UK-UK-UK

Leaving Angar to fire indiscriminately at the misshapen creatures as they cut down members of his team with brutal efficiency.

At least until another sound drowned it all out—the shattering crash of the dome exploding inward.

As the middle ship plunged out of the X formation, leaving a trail of smoke, Tork leaped for the next closest ship, the one above and to starboard...and came up short. He swung the battle axe forward, hoping to sink it into the nearest wing, but it missed.

Tumbling, he settled for the next ship down. His magnetic boots landed behind the V-shaped cockpit, and he steadied himself as the craft bobbed under his weight.

Then, he quickly set about hacking his way inside. Again, occupants jumped out to challenge him, and he made short work of them with his electrified axe.

As he'd done the first time, he hacked away inside the cockpit, tearing up the controls within reach and slaughtering the pilot. Fires broke out in the axe's wake, and he felt the ship dip under him, ready to fall.

Just then, another ship charged toward him, strafing the damaged craft with searing white energy beams. Tork took a running leap and sank his axe in the next ship's nose, then swung his legs up and over the front edge and rolled quickly onto his knees.

This time, no one left the cockpit when he cracked it with his axe. Instead, they fought back by spinning and rolling the ship, trying to shake him.

He held on by his axe during the wild maneuvers, hacking it deep into the fuselage and refusing to let go. He held tight even when the ship turned upside-down, leaving him hanging by a sizzling volcanic vent.

With a cry of effort, he kicked back hard, clamping his magnetic boots onto the hull. With a firm lock on the skin of the ship, he stood upright and continued hacking away.

Soon enough, equipment and people plunged out of the open cockpit. Another ship flashed up, trying to dislodge him, and he dropped onto it, ready to continue his work. He was done with the previous ship, anyway; it spiraled down in his wake, spewing smoke and flame as it barreled toward a bubbling lava flow.

That made three ships down and three to go, counting the one he'd just boarded.

This time, however, the situation changed. Even as Tork hoisted his axe over the cockpit, intending to cause maximum damage, he saw the other two ships glide away.

They stopped some distance away, hovering side-by-side, and the cannons on their wings began to glow. Realizing they were about to open fire, sacrificing one of their own ships to neutralize him, Tork looked around for a quick survival strategy—and came up empty. The ship he was attacking was isolated in the smoky sky, leaving him nowhere to go but hundreds of feet down to the ground below.

In desperation, he hacked away at the cockpit shielding, as if he might somehow be able to operate the controls inside. It was impossible, he'd never flown before, but it was his last option and he had to at least try.

It turned out he didn't need to worry. The two ships fired their weapons elsewhere, blasting away at a point in midair that was midway between them and Tork. The beams from their cannons pulsed red instead of white, and the point where they met flashed and danced like a spark on a lit fuse.

As Tork watched, the spark brightened, blazing so hot, it made him squint. It expanded fast, taking up a bigger and bigger patch of sky, becoming a great burning circle like a fiery hoop.

Then, suddenly, the two ships stopped shooting and lobbed some kind of strobing projectiles at the circle— objects that gave off a wildly flickering light that made them look as if they were flying in a staggered, jittery path.

When the projectiles touched the circle, it flared with blinding light, forcing Tork to look away. When he looked back, he saw the fiery rim of the circle now enclosed a view of another place, like a hole floating in the air.

Like a portal.

Through the opening, Tork saw many more bone white ships like the ones he'd been fighting, moving through a dark sky in a close formation. They looked like they were pushing toward the gap, ready to cross over to Io.

So now Angar knew how seven ships had come to Io instead of the one that had been expected. They must have come through a similar doorway from the same place, a place where other ships were waiting.

And there were *so many* of them over there, he doubted he could defeat them. Six of those ships had been enough of a challenge, let alone a fleet of reinforcements.

Closing the portal and keeping them from coming through was the best strategy—but he had no way to get over there and slam the door shut.

At least until a familiar skiff zoomed up and jolted to a stop in front of him, and a familiar voice called out over the thinklink.

"Sssorry I'm late!" said Valla. "It took me longer than expected to ssscuttle that harrier! I didn't even ssstick around to see it crash because I knew you needed me!"

"Valla!" he shouted. "We need to close that doorway!"

"Then don't just ssstand there, bosss! Get your asss over here! Chop chop!"

35

ANGAR NEVER FELT OVERWHELMED. He was a Horde Lord, a king among men, a conqueror. He was the one who did the overwhelming, never the one who was overwhelmed.

He had seen and done so much in his life, he liked to think nothing truly surprised him. Even the most shocking and brutal atrocities, he had witnessed or performed with his own hands.

Yet there he was, in the middle of utter madness, and he was feeling absolutely overwhelmed.

His teammates were being gunned down by hideous shapeshifting Malignancies. A bone-white spaceship with black and yellow stripes on its wings, engulfed in raging flames from stem to stern, had just crashed through the dome and was rocketing toward the street. The air in the domed station was rushing out through the hole the ship had opened, quickly thinning around him.

And he realized, when he reached for the helmet at his hip, that it had been smashed in the battle.

"Shang." He looked calm as he tossed the helmet aside and watched the flaming ship plunging toward the station buildings—but he wasn't calm at all. For once in his life, he was so far out of his element and under such extreme stress that his usual coping mechanisms and reflexes had short-circuited.

The black-and-yellow winged ship streaked into the high central steeple, exploding against its silver skin. For an instant, it seemed the steeple might hold—but then a second blast rocked it as the remains of the ship blew apart, throwing flaming debris in all directions. The tip of the steeple crumbled first, and then the middle went with it, an avalanche of metal, glass, and concrete cascading toward the street.

That onrushing slide of material was enough to finally snap Angar out of his daze. Heart pounding, he raced away from it, pausing only to scoop up his sword from the blood-strewn street.

Even as he tried to outrun the collapsing spire, slabs of broken glass crashed down from the shattered dome, narrowly missing him. The ground shook, nearly knocking him off his feet, and he had to duck and dodge the streams of projectiles fired by the shapeshifter aliens, which continued to slash through the air.

Then, just as he was about to cross an expanse of street, aiming for the distant airlock, he heard a boom like a thunderbolt, and cracking like an entire forest of trees being splintered at once.

Looking up, he saw fissures racing through a massive section of the dome, then enormous pieces breaking free in a staggering chain reaction. One chunk after another careened downward, slamming into the street with terrible force.

Adrenaline blazed through Angar's bloodstream, compelling him to move, but he didn't know what to do next. If he ran any further forward, the falling slabs could crush him—but the burning, collapsing buildings were deathtraps, too. Nowhere under the dome was safe now, except the airlock.

He decided to make a run for it.

Pain shot through him as hunks of glass pelted him like fist-sized hailstones. A slab the size of the skiff crashed down suddenly in his path, barely missing him as he dodged and sprinted around it. Tremors continued to shake his footing, making it nearly impossible to avoid a fall.

He was halfway to the airlock when the shortness of breath kicked in. He found himself gasping for air as he ran, unable to pull in the deep, full breaths he needed.

His pace slowed, and he started feeling light-headed. He stopped to catch his breath, leaning over in a daze— and a glass slab crashing nearby snapped him out of it. Shaking his head hard, he clawed in what air he could and kept going.

But just as he was almost to the airlock, the street quaked so hard, it threw him down. He landed on his belly and rolled over, intending to leap back up and continue his desperate race.

But then he saw, as a gigantic glittering slab of dome glass slumped toward him, ready to fall, that it was much too late for that.

36

TORK FINISHED HACKING open the cockpit and wrecking the controls of the alien ship, sending it tipping toward the ground. Then, he hopped onto the nose of Valla's skiff and banged the fuselage with the handle of his axe.

"Let's go!" He pointed the blade in the direction of the portal. "Get me over there!"

"And then what, bosss?" Valla's voice in his mind sounded doubtful. "How are we going to ssstop an entire fleet?"

"*We* aren't!" He crouched, bracing himself with the axe handle. "Now go!"

The skiff started moving toward the portal.

"But I ssstill don't know what you want me to do," said Valla. "Other than getting you over there."

"Take out the two ships that opened the doorway," said Tork. "Make sure they can't do it again."

"But what about you, bosss? What's going to happen to *you?*"

"I'll take my place in the Never-Ending War, probably."
Glaring at the portal, he tensed every muscle in his body,
getting ready. "But I won't go alone, I'll tell you that."

"But bosss," said Valla. "I can't jussst let you..."

"We only have *seconds* until those ships sail through!"
he snapped. "Now *go!*"

Was it possible for a Sisslak to sob? Tork thought he
heard such a sound from the cockpit, though he couldn't
be sure.

Then, the skiff speeded up, aiming dead on at its
target.

Valla came in with guns blazing, spewing slugs of
superheated plasma at the two ships that had opened the
portal. The ships responded by launching a barrage of
energy beams, blasting away from either side of the fiery
doorway.

As the beams slashed past and the skiff flung him
forward, Tork centered his mind and heart, preparing for
what was coming.

The fleet had to be stopped, and there was no one
around but him to do it. If those ships got through and
took the fight to Earth, it could mean the end of everything he cared about.

Not for the first time in his life, he had no choice. The
future rested on the Horde Lord's shoulders; it was up to
him to rise to the occasion.

For a moment, then, time seemed to slow down for
him. The portal grew larger as he approached it, the shim-
mering vision of the ships on the other side becoming
ever clearer.

How he wished that doorway could return him to his

life on Earth again. If only his people awaited on the other side, smiling and waving and reaching. He missed that world, which was so far away now—and about to get even farther, he suspected.

Just before the skiff got him close enough, then, he thought of Angar. For once, he thought of him not with loathing or rage or revulsion. He simply wondered if he'd ever see him again after this.

He wondered also if the blowback effect between them had been switched off as Angar had predicted. If it wasn't, and Tork died in his jump, would Angar die, too?

Then, Tork took a deep breath and leaped. Arms outspread, axe extended, he dove into the portal, gliding like an eagle toward the waiting fleet of ships.

Just as he crossed the threshold, he felt a strange shortness of breath. Was the portal affecting his breathing somehow, in spite of his helmet and functioning air supply?

With one last gasp, he was gone.

The rim of the portal flickered as he entered, then collapsed seconds later as Valla destroyed the two ships that had opened it in the first place.

"Bosss?" called Valla over the thinklink. "Tork? Do you read me?"

The only thing that came back to her was mental static. The only movement she saw was from the columns of fire and smoke dancing from the sizzling vents below.

SOMEHOW, as the massive slab of dome glass teetered over Angar, he finally caught his breath.

It was as if someone had breathed fresh air directly into him, filling his lungs. His head cleared instantly, and his muscles stopped aching.

He didn't understand. The dome was wide open to the airless outside...but it didn't matter.

Rolling to his knees, he grabbed his sword from the street and burst into a run, sprinting as fast as he could from the area under the slab.

When it broke all the way free and fell, crashing down with a thunderous boom, he was in the clear, barely. Shards peppered him as he ran, and a few big pieces slammed into his back and legs, but he hadn't been crushed or punctured or sliced to ribbons by the glass.

His breathing came easily now, without effort. He made the most of it, running for the airlock. Even if he was breathing fine, the airlock was the quickest way out of Io Station, out of the path of the collapsing dome.

But just as he was nearly there, the ground shook so hard it knocked him down again. A loud rumbling rolled through the station, and more sections of the dome cracked and fell.

There was a tremendous roar from beyond the dome, and he looked up to see a new volcano had forced its way up and exploded. Showers of red lava sprayed from the newborn cone, and he could see it was going to land nearby.

Even as the eruption continued, rivers of lava from the volcano melted their way through the base of the dome and flowed inward, glowing and bubbling. Everything caught in their path was quickly dissolved, from the street to the shapeshifters to the slabs of dome glass. Some of his own people were in jeopardy, too, battle survivors like Schist and Demagorn who were trapped by the fallen floes of glass.

As Angar got up, he saw there was no way he could get to the survivors. There was nothing anyone could do to help any of them at that point.

Then, suddenly, he heard another sound overhead, a deep, familiar rumble. A shadow glided over him from beyond the disintegrating dome, the shadow of something huge—and he looked up.

And there it was. A colossal death's head, glowing with crimson light, was passing into the airspace above Io Station.

The *Hellcyon* had arrived.

As soon as he saw it, the voice of Finn Gauge reverberated in his head, speaking over the thinklink. "Everyone stand by. We're picking you all up immediately."

Angar watched as the immense bulk of the *Hellcyon* slid overhead. Winged silver rescue pods dropped from its belly like pearls, escorted by the great black dragon ship he and Tork had battled on Earth, belching flame from its maw to light the way.

The pods swooped into the space inside the broken dome, heading for the battleground...but Angar wondered if they'd made a wasted trip. How many of his team were even still alive to pick up?

He was ashamed to admit he didn't know. He almost wished the *Hellcyon* hadn't gotten there at all.

Because then the Blacksmiths would never know how overwhelmed he'd been...and, in the end, how he'd done the one thing he'd done only once before, when Scalder Pacious had perished and the Grand and Glorious Horde had been conquered on his watch.

He'd failed.

"Angar?" Another voice spoke in his mind, then, sweet and melodic. "I'm coming to pick you up."

The thought of Quinza being near should have soothed him, but it didn't. When her pod landed in front of him and opened, revealing her sitting inside, he actually felt a little worse. Even more than the rest of the *Hellcyon*'s crew, he didn't want her to see the disaster he'd failed to stop.

"You need a *helmet!*" She looked down from the hovering pod with an alarmed expression—then turned and grabbed a spare helmet from inside the pod.

As she hopped down into the rubble, the wings of her

butterflies fluttered under her own helmet. She ran to him, ready to clamp the spare helmet over his head—and then she stopped and stared with amazement.

"Are you *breathing?*" She tipped her head to one side. "Without a *helmet?*"

"Don't tell anyone," he said over the thinklink, and then he took the helmet from her and put it on. "Please? Not until I figure it all out."

"All right." Reaching over, she tightened the helmet's seal and connected the air supply on his back to the feeder hose. "So you really *are* a mystery, aren't you, Angar Crux?"

Suddenly, the ground shook with the force of another eruption. Lava bombs crashed into the sections of the dome that were still standing, and the superheated flow on the ground moved faster, sliding toward them.

"Come on!" Quinza helped him to the pod. "Unless you have a death wish, we need to get out of her *now.*"

He hesitated, considering what she'd said. Letting the lava consume him would be one way to avoid dealing with his failure.

Then Quinza tugged at his sleeve, and he fell in step beside her. As much as he hated what had happened on Io, going with her still made him feel better.

Though not for long.

As she flew him back to the *Hellcyon*, a strange feeling swept through him, unlike anything he had ever experienced before. It made him gasp out loud and twist in his seat, straining to make it go away.

But it wouldn't.

"Are you all right?" Quinza sounded deeply concerned.

His heart hammered like the hoofbeats of a stampede of horses. "Fine, I'm fine." Even as he said it, strange waves rippled through him, pulling him...*elsewhere.* A force he'd never felt before flared in his chest and head, lighting him up with an awareness of incredible distance, a trail leading through it...

...and someone waiting at the other end of it like a beacon.

"Are you sure you're okay?" asked Quinza. "It sounded like you were in pain."

Angar took a deep breath and let it out slowly. His heart was returning to a normal rhythm, and the waves flowing through him were not so overwhelming anymore.

"I'm okay, thanks," he told her. "Everything's good."

But he still sensed a trail through trackless space. And that presence like a beacon at the end of it.

EPILOGUE

"Tork is gone," said Isabel. "Gone without a trace."

Those gathered in the Cortex of the *Hellcyon* listened grimly. Hours had passed since the battle on Io, and the bad news just kept coming.

Though the latest announcement should have been *good* news for Angar. All his life, he had fought for one goal—the annihilation of his hated enemy, Tork Gallgore. It was the one true driving force behind everything he'd done, the dream that had seen him through countless wars and struggles and challenges. Hearing it had finally been accomplished should have filled him to overflowing with absolute joy, a feeling of destiny fulfilled.

But he felt none of that.

"I wish I hadn't closed the portal." Valla, who stood near the center of the Cortex, sounded regretful. "Or at leassst, I should have found a way to go in after him."

"You did the right thing," said Gauge. "For the good of the solar system and our homeworld."

"Maybe so." Punji's petals fluttered with agitation. "But where does that leave us and our vaunted plans?"

"Nothing changes," said Gauge.

"Are you kidding me?" Punji snorted out a cloud of pollen. "We lost six of our shipmates on Io. Tork, our *other* great barbarian hope, is who-knows-where. And *all* the residents of Io Station have *disappeared*! Not a single one of them, alive or dead, was left on Io after the Caul incursion. You don't think that *changes* things?"

"Of course it does," said Gauge. "It means it's more vital than ever that we accomplish our plans."

"The people we lost would have done the same if the roles were reversed," said Isabel. "They would have been more determined than *ever* to defeat the enemy." She smacked her fist in the palm of her hand. "We can't let their sacrifice have been for nothing."

"We won't," said Gauge. "We won't let the loss of Tork stop us. We desperately needed Tork, but Angar will just have to take up the mantle for both of them."

With that, all eyes turned to Angar, who stood at the furthest fringe of the Cortex.

"What do you say, Horde Lord?" asked Gauge. "Are you ready to accept the challenge? Are you ready to be the sole champion of humanity and our allies in the war to come?"

Angar scowled. The words should have thrilled him. The outcome was perfectly in line with his plans from the start—that he would subjugate these Blacksmiths and their science and use them to realize his own vision of conquest among the stars. Everything was working out perfectly for him.

But Angar couldn't revel in this success, because he knew the truth.

He hesitated, because revealing what he knew went against everything he'd lived for. It would be an act of self-sabotage, as well, wrecking the very plans he was on the verge of fulfilling.

But the feeling deep inside him wouldn't go away...the sure and certain knowledge that somewhere out there like a distant beacon, far beyond Io, beyond even the solar system...

"Tork is alive." Even as the words left his lips, he doubted he should say them. But then there was no going back.

Gauge frowned. "What do you mean, he's alive?"

"I can feel it." Angar tapped the side of his head with an index finger. "Somehow...the connection between us...I can *feel* him."

"Through the blowback link, you mean?" asked Isabel. "You feel second-hand pain through the link?"

"Not pain, no. I felt no pain from him during the mission." It had been just as Angar had predicted, that blowback would be disabled during the battle. But what he *hadn't* predicted were the echoes of Tork that kept coming back to him now from whatever great beyond he'd ended up in. The same signal he'd first received in the escape pod with Quinza had kept repeating without fluc-tuation ever since.

"You sense he's alive, but not in pain?" said Gauge.

"Yes," said Angar.

"Are you sure you can't tell us more about where he

is?" asked Isabel. "Is he somewhere on the surface of Io, perhaps?"

"Not on Io." Angar shook his head. "He's *out there* somewhere." He gestured at the starscape through the transparent ceiling, all the points of light glittering against the velvety black backdrop. "I can't explain it, but I can *feel* him, like a beacon."

"Well, that narrows it down," said Punji.

"What else can you tell us?" asked Gauge.

Angar shrugged. "Nothing."

"And you can definitely *feel* him out there somehow?" asked Isabel. "Do you think you could *find* him?"

Again, Angar stood on the verge of decision. If he denied this, he could still fulfill his life's dream and stick with his plans.

But he didn't. "Yes. I think I can find him."

Even as he said it, he knew why. Because in spite of everything else, he knew things were different than he'd thought at first. *He* was different.

He could breathe on the surface of an airless moon. He could sense the life force of his fellow Horde Lord across unimaginable distances.

And the Blacksmiths wouldn't tell him why. Only one other person might be able to help him understand and put his abilities to use. One other person who shared those powers and more. He knew it; he could *feel* it.

Just as the Blacksmiths needed Tork, Angar needed him, too...at least until he mastered this situation.

"All right then." Gauge nodded. "Let's see what we can do about that. Let's see if we can find him."

"And face the Caul fleet on the other side of that portal," said Isabel.

"It does make sense to confront that force, wherever it is," said Gauge. "If we find that fleet, we find the jumping-off point for the Caul's invasion of our solar system."

"Maybe we'll find more than that," said Punji. "Maybe we'll bite off more than we can chew."

"So be it." Gauge clapped his hands together. "We'll see if we can track Tork, then. We'll see where that road takes us. But first..." He turned to Lieutenant Jelani at the helm station. "Get us back to Earth. Top speed, Eshe."

"Earth?" Isabel frowned.

"As originally planned, we need to pick up some reinforcements." Gauge looked at Angar. "A certain horde you might be familiar with."

Angar's eyes widened.

"We need an army if we're taking on the Caul," said Gauge. "Do you think you can help get them ready for the fight?"

Angar smiled. Though he'd gone against his instincts and desires, things were coming together after all.

He'd been in over his head for a while, overwhelmed, but he felt himself rising at last. There was hope, after all, that he could triumph in ways he'd never imagined.

"Let's talk on the way home," said Gauge. "You and I, Angar. Tell me what we can do to prepare your people and win the war."

Angar's hand tightened on the hilt of his sword. Lightning flashed in his mind. Thunder boomed in his heart.

He would spare these people for now, as he had spared

others before them. But their usefulness, and their control over him, would not last forever.

His mercy, the mercy of a Horde Lord, was as fleeting as the stroke of a blood-soaked blade, and twice again as unpredictable.

TO BE CONTINUED IN *STARBARIAN SAGA BOOK 2: HORDE'S POWER!*

ABOUT THE AUTHOR

Robert Jeschonek is an envelope-pushing, *USA Today* best-selling author whose fiction, comics, and non-fiction have been published around the world. His stories have appeared in *Clarkesworld, Galaxy's Edge, StarShipSofa, Pulphouse,* and many other publications. He has written official *Star Trek* and *Doctor Who* fiction and has scripted comics for DC, AHOY, and others. His young adult slipstream novel, *My Favorite Band Does Not Exist*, won the Forward National Literature Award and was named one of *Booklist's* Top Ten First Novels for Youth. He also won an International Book Award, a Scribe Award for Best Original Novel, and the grand prize in Pocket Books' Strange New Worlds contest. Visit him online at www.bobscribe.-com. You can also find him on Facebook and follow him as @TheFictioneer on Twitter.

From "The Stars So Black, The Space So White"

Imagine standing in the prow of a great sailing vessel, gazing out at the starry darkness as it folds around the nose of the ship. Now imagine the ship is in space.

And you are standing on an onyx gangplank, a sheer, black surface reflecting the starlight all around--creating the illusion that you are suspended without support in the void. Exposed to the nip and tug of so many rays and waves and streams and particles, yet somehow protected.

Watch as crackling suns and jewel-like worlds spin past. Wonder at the feathery, pastel tendrils of glowing nebulae. Grin with delight, because no matter how many times you see this, you can't help but marvel.

I can't help but marvel.

Welcome to my life. From Earthbound bartender savant to crewman on an alien spacecraft. From man of 20th century Earth to man of the cosmos.

You wish you were me. You *totally* wish you were me.

"I should have known." The voice behind me is high-pitched and piping with a fluttery vibrato. "I would find you here. Rudeee Tabernacle."

Turning, I smile at the dozens of multifaceted silver eyes staring my way, twisting on the ends of pale yellow tendrils. The tendrils are rooted in a glittering, creamy cloud, a misty blur of ever-shifting size and shape that hovers a meter above the onyx gangplank. Who knew I could come to love and respect someone so alien?

Who knew I could come to see my *abductor* as my *friend*?

"You are not feeling. Worried, are you?" The voice

emanates from somewhere in the cloud. It's the same voice I first heard fifty years ago, asking a question that changed my life forever and led me to this moment.

"Only hopeful." I bow, as is the custom in the fleet of the civilization whose name translates as The Rising. After fifty years among The Rising (though I look half as old as that, thanks to alien rejuvenation techniques), I know all the right things to do and say...though I don't always do and say them. But that, too, is customary; it's part of my job, after all.

They call me a *Chancer*. An X-factor in a social hierarchy with too much order...and a need for controlled chaos in the face of a highly improvisational universe.

As for the alien, if you called him/her/it/them a captain/teacher/lama/inexplicable presence, you wouldn't be wrong. "We approach. The source of. The signal."

His/her/its/their actual name is unpronounceable for a human like me, so I go with a boiled-down nickname. "Most Eager, has the content of the signal changed?"

Most Eager hiss-cough-squeals in a way that equates to a human head-shake. "The signal continues. To repeat."

I know the message by heart by now. "*Black stars. White space. Forever screaming.*"

"We will be there. Soon, Rudeee. The..." He calls our giant vessel by the name its builders gave it, which translates like this (more or less): *Peacefaring Manyfold Transitory Translightenment Construct, Constant.* "...will arrive within. The hour."

I shorten the ship's name like always. "The *Transit*'s ready, Most Eager. We'll do what we do best."

"Answer questions." Most Eager stiffens all

his/her/its/their tendrils at once like stalks in a cornfield. It's a salute. "Save lives."

I answer with a salute of my own, holding both fists at shoulder height, opening them into flattened palms. "And set the stage for tomorrow."

Setting the stage is The Rising's truest mission, our reason for being among the stars in the first place. The galaxy is full of lifeforms in varying degrees of evolution; we create mysteries that will draw them out here when the time is right to join the community of starfaring beings.

Speaking of mysteries, a ship like our own comes into view up ahead--a cluster of giant black shapeshifting objects, spherical at the moment like a bunch of grapes or a clutch of atoms in a molecule. The spheres, which normally blink with multicolored lights, are dark--and cut in half down the middle, wedged in a swirling halo of bright blue light.

"Do you think. They are still. Alive?" asks Most Eager.

I know he/she/it/they can tell if I'm lying, but I do it anyway. "Of course." After all, he/she/it/they has/have kin on that vessel.

More than kin. More like a protégé beloved above all others. And a *human*, like me.

Her name is Julie. And it is *her* voice--the voice of the trapped ship's first officer--repeating that message, over and over:

"Black stars. White space. Forever screaming."

～

What happens next? Find out in Blastoff!, *now available for your favorite e-reading device or app!*